The
Extinction
of Desire

A Tale of Enlightenment

Blackwell Public Philosophy
Edited by Michael Boylan, Marymount University

In a world of 24-hour news cycles and increasingly specialized knowledge, the Blackwell Public Philosophy series takes seriously the idea that there is a need and demand for engaging and thoughtful discussion of topics of broad public importance. Philosophy itself is historically grounded in the public square, bringing people together to try to understand the various issues that shape their lives and give them meaning. This "love of wisdom" – the essence of philosophy – lies at the heart of the series. Written in an accessible, jargon-free manner by internationally renowned authors, each book is an invitation to the world beyond newsflashes and soundbites and into public wisdom.

For further information about individual titles in the series, supplementary material, and regular updates, visit www.blackwellpublishing.com/publicphilosophy.

Blackwell
Publishing

The
Extinction
of Desire

A Tale of Enlightenment

MICHAEL BOYLAN

BLACKWELL PUBLISHING
350 Main Street, Malden, MA 02148-5020, USA
9600 Garsington Road, Oxford OX4 2DQ, UK
550 Swanston Street, Carlton, Victoria 3053, Australia

First published 2007 by Blackwell Publishing Ltd

This a work of fiction. Names, characters, and incidents are the product of the author's
imagination, and any resemblance to actual persons, living or dead, is entirely coincidental.

1   2007

Library of Congress Cataloging-in-Publication Data

Boylan, Michael, 1952–
    The extinction of desire : a tale of enlightenment / Michael Boylan.
        p. cm. — (Blackwell public philosophy)
    ISBN-13: 978-1-4051-4849-8 (hardback: acid-free paper)
    ISBN-13: 978-1-4051-4850-4 (paperback: acid-free paper)
    1. Wealth—Moral and ethical aspects—Fiction.   2. Conduct of life—Fiction.
    3. Buddhism—Fiction.   I. Title

PS3552.L27E96 2007
813'.6—dc22

                                                        2006035619

A catalogue record for this title is available from the British Library.

Set in 11.5 on 14 pt Dante
by SNP Best-set Typesetter Ltd, Hong Kong
Printed and bound in Singapore
by Markono Print Media Pte Ltd

The publisher's policy is to use permanent paper from mills that operate a sustainable
forestry policy, and which has been manufactured from pulp processed using acid-free and
elementary chlorine-free practices. Furthermore, the publisher ensures that the text paper
and cover board used have met acceptable environmental accreditation standards.

For further information on
Blackwell Publishing, visit our website:
www.blackwellpublishing.com

Contents

The Four Noble Truths
Sarvam Duhkha: All is suffering
Trishna: Desire is the cause of suffering
Nirvana: The extinction of desire liberates one from suffering
Madhyamarga: The direction to follow is the Eightfold Path

Foreword

Charles Johnson

After reading philosopher Michael Boylan's entertaining and thought-provoking philosophical narrative, *The Extinction of Desire*, I found myself thinking of the real-life morality tale of Andrew Jackson Whittaker Jr., a 57-year-old native of Charleston, West Virginia, who in 2004 won the largest undivided lottery in the history of the United States: a Powerball jackpot worth $314 million. This good fortune, or so some claimed, was the American Dream of material prosperity come true, and Whittaker donated $20 million of his new-found wealth to various charities. But within two years this dream of winning "the cosmic lotto" and finding "a way to beat one's karma," as Boylan so beautifully describes the addiction to betting, transformed into a terrifying modern-day Buddhist parable. In August 2003, a strip club owner and his girlfriend were charged with drugging Whittaker and stealing from his SUV a briefcase containing $545,000 in cash and checks. In March of the next year, his SUV was broken into again, and a thief stole $100 in a bank bag. His office was broken into – on that occasion $2,000 was taken. Then his home was broken into on the day the dead body of an 18-year-old boy, a friend of his granddaughter Brandi Lasha Bragg, was discovered on the premises. (Some claimed she supplied the boy with drugs purchased with money Whittaker gave her.) By March of 2006, his granddaughter was missing. Two years earlier, an employee at a race track and casino alleged that Whittaker sexually assaulted her. By December of 2004, he had been arrested twice for drunken driving and ordered to enter rehab for a 28-day period. He also faced charges for attacking a bar manager. In 2006, Whittaker's wife Jewel told the *Charleston Gazette* that, "I wish all of this had never happened. I wish I would have torn the ticket up."

Perhaps these days Jack Whittaker is pondering the question asked in the opening sentence of *The Extinction of Desire*, "What would you do if you suddenly became rich?" In the case of this novel's protagonist, Michael O'Meara, a Fairview High School teacher in Bethesda, Maryland, the sudden windfall involved – $1 million received after a freak accident wipes out his family, leaving him the only heir – is miniscule compared to Whittaker's, but that seven-figure sum is enough to trigger a destabilizing "chain reaction" in which, he says, "I found myself confronted with myself. And I wasn't really prepared for that." In other words, he must critically examine his "worldview," a key concept in Boylan's writings as a professional philosopher. In that analytic context, he says of the Personal Worldview Imperative that, "All people must develop a single comprehensive and internally coherent worldview that is good and that we strive to act out in our daily lives." The plot and broad cast of characters in *The Extinction of Desire* pressure O'Meara to wonder, "Was it my own tattered worldview that was ready for collapse?" The answer is yes, but his achieving a new one, far from taking place in a comfortable classroom setting, can only be arrived at through an outer and inner journey into what phenomenologists have referred to as the *Lebenswelt* ("Life-world"), of unpredictably dangerous real people, real things, and real places.

For in the best philosophical fiction, ideas do not float disembodied far above human experience in a remote (or immanent) Platonic realm of forms, abstracted from what Ch'an (Zen) Buddhists would call the everydayness of life. On the contrary: engaging philosophical fiction returns intellectual questions to their place of origin, which is the muck and mud and sweaty messiness, the ambiguity of lived experience so overrich in meaning prior to our truncating explanations and the Procrustean beds of our theories. Then the novelist dramatizes these experiences and ideas captured in their "wild being" (as philosopher Maurice Merleau-Ponty once put it) in a process that has epistemological importance insofar as new, hitherto unseen or concealed profiles (meanings) of the phenomenon may be revealed – a disclosure not unlike the revelation O'Meara encounters in the story about Zen Buddhist nun Chiyono when the bottom falls out of her old pail bound with bamboo. Our perception or way of seeing is forever changed. Thus, as a *dramatic narrative*, a well-crafted philosophical novel (or any novel) is never a series of dry lectures, or academic dialogues. Characters do not sit in a parlor sipping Chardonnay and dispassionately discussing ideas. They must *live* them, and for high stakes. They must dramatically face what Sartre called "the agony of choice." Ideas must be tabernacled in the rich possibilities of character and event. And when this is masterfully accomplished, a reader is enriched by the *re*-incarnation of ideas, by imaginative storytelling giving abstractions flesh and palpability.

The experiential topography of Michael O'Meara's Life-world is presented early in the story by a nameless, gum-chewing girl at Fairview High eager to marry a rich Georgetown law student. But, she says, "I won't stay married to him. Oh no. I'm too smart for that. I'll divorce him and take half his money . . . To have *me* it's going to *cost* him." Although probably a poor student academically, this young gold-digger understands the "ethos centered around the acquisition of *things*," which is universally grounded in the basic goods required for human action – food, clothing, shelter, and protection from bodily harm. Most likely, she is not a "bad" person, but the urge to not only survive but also prosper – as a tactic for dealing with everyone's dread of poverty and death – leads to a Hobbesian state that exacerbates ruthless competition and inequality: a social realm we know all too well today because many residents of non-Western nations live on a dollar a day (or less), and here in America, which consumes the lion's share of the world's resources, citizens are bombarded with 3,000 product messages a day (according to Brad Adgate, senior vice-president of the New York branding firm Horizon Media) that enflame and condition (if not actually create) an endless amount of thirst for (*trishna* in Sanskrit) and attachment to *things*. That ethos has also been internalized by O'Meara's ex-wife Sara. A woman who reduces herself and others to a state of thinghood, and yearns to "be with the 'important' people and collect desirable acquaintances so they might be displayed for all to see," she demands more alimony and child support (for children from her earlier marriage) after learning of Michael's inheritance. Like the tiger raised as a grass-eating goat in the novel's prologue, almost everyone in O'Meara's world – from his swindling college friend Bernie to the "honest crook" Mookie – discovers their "true nature" is, if not predatory, then certainly dominated by the acquisitive profit-motive, by "overreaching for what you don't have." That, for Hobbes, is the primary sin, as the protagonist learns late in the story. And this sin appears in Boylan's philosophy as the violation of two requirements for any civilized society: namely, "the assurance that those you interact with are not lying to promote their own interests," and "the assurance that those you interact with will recognize your human dignity and not exploit you as a means only."

Yet O'Meara, the poor scholar, is still something of a grass-grazing goat when the novel begins, and therefore he is at a disadvantage in this loveless realm of greed, conspicuous consumption, and selfishness. He is still grieving for his dead father, and longing for his "quasi fiancée" Aisling, his Beatrice, who has left her teaching post at Fairview High to complete her doctorate at the University of London. All in all, O'Meara is charmingly quirky in his morality, believing that, "You can't be perfect. You shouldn't even try to be perfect . . . The Turkish rug makers used to have a tradition of putting a flaw in each of their rugs . . . To show to God that they did not aspire to perfection.

The very thought would have been an instance of pride." In a social world of movers and shakers, O'Meara – so lacking in vanity, so flawed – is usually the "shaken," a man lacking "inner fire. . . . Reactive and not proactive" was his style. However, once wealth comes, he dabbles in a received, unearned worldview, which produces moral dilemmas that only deepen his state of disequilibrium.

Those scenes in *The Extinction of Desire* when O'Meara tries his best to be a winner and stop being "screwed, blued, and tattooed" by others, are deliciously ironic moments of comedy. Aware that Bernie has invested his windfall in a shady operation called Capital Ventures in "a Ponzi fraud with new monies used to cover old debts," O'Meara's only recourse is to correct a deceit with a deceit of his own by taking out a loan from a subsidiary of Capital Ventures and *not* repaying it. He toys with purchasing luxury items such as an imitation Patek Phillippe watch, feeling, "I would not be honest if I didn't . . . find *something* attractive about these baubles. But what was it? How strong was its force? Would it win me over, too?" For a time, he acquires a BMW and a three-leveled "behemoth" of a house, but eventually this flirtation with the hedonistic fantasy of a "pampered life" abruptly ends when O'Meara finds himself thrown into a German jail.

There, he encounters cellmates who represent three of the classic "Four Signs" of impermanence and change – old age, sickness, and death – that all life will inevitably experience. That transitoriness includes thoughts as well as things, and is summarized in the terse Pali formulation *anicca duhkah anatta* ("All things are transitory; there is suffering; and there is no enduring self"). According to legend, these signs of the brevity (*anicca*) and ontological emptiness (*shunyata*) of all things led Indian prince Siddhartha Gautama to abandon the pleasure palace of his father to pursue spiritual awakening. No matter how wealthy or famous people may become, O'Meara sees, these three signs will spoil their ephemeral pleasures (*duhkah*) and heaped-up possessions (or, as a friend of mine puts it, "You've never seen a hearse carrying luggage, have you?"), and they will, if they are observant, appreciate how in a world where all things are mutually dependent and interconnected (*pratitya samutpada*), the idea of an independent, separate, enduring self or individuality is simply an illusion (*anatta*).

In that jail cell, O'Meara does not see the fourth sign, a wise and holy man whose tranquility suggested to young Siddhartha that perhaps there might be a path one could pursue to achieve release from the suffering caused by the first three conditions. (For one of his epigraphs, Boylan recites that canonical Buddhist blueprint or path for enlightenment and liberation called the "Four Noble Truths," the last of these truths being that liberation is realized by following "The Eight-Fold Path," or *Arya Ashtanga Marga*.) The reason for that omission is because during O'Meara's journey he has already come to know two important avatars ready to assist his developing a new worldview. The first is his priest, Father Mac, a man who appreciates the life of the senses without becoming lost in it. "Quality things in life that give us pleasure should not be rejected out of hand," he says. "The Lord gave us whiskey and fine watches and other trinkets to satisfy our longing for perfection which is only understood in the abstract through God . . . it's not the trinkets themselves that are troublesome, but our attitudes about them." In other words, desire and attachment to them make us their slaves.

His second guru is Aisling, a woman of such idealism and integrity that O'Meara remembers her risking her job when their department chair at Fairview High tried to pressure her into passing a failing student because he had a rich, influential father. "I don't care if his father is president of the world," she says. "It has nothing to do with my judging his son's work . . . I stand by my decision." It is, therefore, logical that *The Extinction of Desire*, in addition to being a spirited philosophical odyssey, is also the love story of O'Meara and Aisling. She never tried to "remake me," he says, and her balance and clarity "brought out the best in me." One of the notable accomplishments of Boylan's novel lies in its dramatizing the timeless truth that after awakening (or *nirvana*, which literally means "to blow out" the illusory sense of self or ego) all that remains is a life – and social relations – based on joy, thanksgiving, and love. In the Buddhist tradition this is known as the attitude of *metta* (loving-kindness) toward all sentient beings. Such wisdom is obviously not exclusive to any one culture, Eastern or Western, but rather is – to paraphrase William Faulkner's Nobel Prize acceptance speech – the treasure that awaits all of us when the human heart is no longer in conflict with itself, when the secular and sacred are experienced as one, and when objects and others again radiate a sense of the holy. That, I believe, is a conclusion with which the best novelists and philosophers can agree.

(Charles Johnson, the S. Wilson and Grace M. Pollock Professor for Excellence in English at the University of Washington in Seattle, is the author of *Middle Passage*, winner of the 1990 National Book Award.)

Prologue: An Ancient Fable

His mother died soon after he was born. Somehow he survived. The tiger cub was found by a herd of mountain goats. They took him in and raised him as a goat.

At first it was very hard for him. He had to learn to eat grass with his sharp teeth. His teeth tore at the blades of grass and were not efficient. Soon, however, he ate grass just like the goats. He became quiet and peaceful in his soul as he discovered his bodhi nature.

Then one day he encountered a group of tigers roaming the mountains. They took one look at him and laughed. "What is a tiger doing eating nothing but grass! This is not what tigers are meant to do! Come with us and we will reveal to you your true nature." And so he went.

After a short while the group of tigers came upon a cow wandering at the foot of a mountain. The tigers killed the cow and brought some meat over to the tiger cub. "Here, this is what tigers eat!"

So he ate. The blood and warm flesh made his head spin. Deep inside him something stirred. From some unknown place within came strength. He roared.

The other tigers smiled in delight. "You see. What you were *before* was not your true self. You were duped. Now you have discovered your true nature."

The young tiger became aggressive and thirsty for more fresh meat. He pawed the ground, looked to the west, and eagerly awaited the next kill.

Part One

Chapter One

What would you do if you suddenly became rich?

I'll tell you what I did. It may interest you. You see, I was a high school teacher (or *am* a high school teacher – I'm not sure it ever leaves your blood). I was teaching history at the time, a nebulous discipline that gets civics, geography, psychology, and whatever else dumped into it. I suppose this means history either is the all-encompassing discipline or is nothing whatsoever and so demands continual supplement. But I'm getting away from "the event."

The facts are these. My uncle Will's wife's parents were celebrating their golden wedding anniversary near West Palm Beach, Florida, when a plane crashed into their festivities and killed the lot of them. I wasn't there. I had to work, although no one would have expected me to be at the party. Even my dad had considered skipping it (since going to one's brother's wife's family's get-together is, by any estimation, a bit outlandish). But you see the Tristys were short on family members of their own and so had to import some. My dad humored his baby brother, and Uncle Dick, the eldest, tagged along too.

So there it was: eight people wiped out in a flaming instant, including my father and his two brothers. No heirs except me. It happened on April 1, 1989. No joke. Almost a year and a half later, what with estates, life insurance, and triple indemnity, I was confronted with an item that would change my life: a check for one million dollars.

Now, I know what you're thinking: "A million dollars isn't what it used to be." It is true that in 1960 there were only a few thousand millionaires in the whole country, and now they seem to be as common as cute expressions on T-shirts. But a million dollars is still a lot of money. Or so my friends keep telling me.

"Naturally, you'll let me manage it for you," said Bernie.

"Naturally," I echoed without thinking. Bernie had volunteered to handle my finances. We'd both gone to Pembroke College in Minnesota and now found ourselves living in the Washington, DC, area (albeit he was in a big house near Chevy Chase Circle, and I was in a one-bedroom apartment a few blocks from school).

Bernie was a "take charge" guy. "There's not a moment to lose," he said. "I'll draw up some papers. Now, let's see when I can get them to you. We have a big hearing at the Labor Department tomorrow, so I'm afraid you'll have to wait until Wednesday – unless that's too late. We could meet after work around seven-thirty."

"Wednesday is fine. Thursday is fine. Really, Bernie, there's no rush."

"That's where you're wrong, old salt."

When he wasn't calling me "old salt," Bernie called me "Mike" even though I had told him I preferred "Michael." All my friends call me Michael. Nobody calls me Mike – except if you count Sara. But I'd rather not count her.

"There are taxes and the investment objectives to discuss. You can't accept such a large sum of money responsibly without a plan."

"Right, Bernie."

Bernie was bursting from his vest. His large body reminded me of Father McGinnis, how his belly stuck out like a balloon from the lower abdomen. The difference was that Bernie cultivated his rotund figure to display contented "good living" (which meant "rich living").

Bernie nodded his head and smiled while shuffling papers back into the "file" he'd created for my case. His smile changed his entire face – from the dimples around his eyes to the tautness under his chin. I couldn't help thinking at that moment of how he was when we were at college. He wore his hair long (as everyone did then) and sported a Fu Manchu mustache, which gave him a definite counterculture air. That mustache was his only social link.

Bernie's college-age warm smile was now a taut, knowing grimace. His youthful baby face had been replaced by a topography studded with growths of various elevations. Now he wore his hair medium short and combed straight back, and his clean-shaven visage sometimes reminded me of a Mafia boss.

We shook hands. Bernie's head was still nodding.

What amazed me was how fast the news spread. I hadn't told anyone but Bernie. People at work learned about my father's death when I took time off for the funeral. But nothing was said about the inheritance. Who'd think about that at a funeral?

Well, maybe they do. I did, to the extent that I knew I was my father's only heir. My mom died twenty-three years ago, and my brother was a statistic of Vietnam. I knew I'd get the family pictures and whatever was in the bank account – much as I knew that every so often I had to clean the house. It was necessary for the order of things.

But I'm not very good with money. I readily admit that, every month, my paycheck does not cover my expenses. I'm always about a hundred short. (And that's in a good month!) If I didn't get extra bucks for coaching track and cross-country, or the occasional income from moonlighting at the hardware store as a clerk, I wouldn't be able to pay my bills.

"Oh Michael!" The voice was distinctly Angie's. She has one of those voices that is in between pitches so that you hear it wherever you are.

I turned around and saw her hurrying toward me across the campus. She was managing a load of books and student papers in one arm and tugging at her overstretched vintage dark-brown v-neck sweater with the other – so she wouldn't bounce out. Above her the trees had turned a golden yellow. Soon the leaves would fall. I stopped and watched her approach. Her class was in the other direction.

"I just heard the news," she said when she reached me.

I didn't get it. Angie was always "hearing the news." She had a way of altering her bony nose so that it might fit into everyone's affairs.

"You're rich."

"Rich?"

"Come on. Don't deny it."

I smiled.

"When are you going to quit?"

"I beg your pardon?"

"Quit. Finito. Say 'bye-bye.'"

My lips tightened. I tried turning away. Angie grabbed my arm with her free hand. The tight grip relaxed and transformed itself into gentle stroking. She moved close to me so that my knee was touching her thigh. "You know, now that Ash is away . . ." The bell rang for class.

I opened my mouth but didn't say anything. I couldn't look her in the eye. "I gotta go." It was time for World Civilization.

Maybe it was my imagination, but I began to think that my students were treating me differently, too. It was as if I were now somehow important. On a par with *them*.

Fairview High School students live in a world of money. When you go to the parking lot, it isn't hard to tell students' cars from faculty's. The former are new, shining, and upscale. The latter are smaller, older, and out of fashion. This is not the way I remember it, growing up in Evanston, Illinois. Most students didn't have cars, and those who did drove "handy-man specials."

You can imagine how hard it is to motivate students who know that, no matter how they do in school, a nice job will be waiting for them via mommy and daddy's influence. College tuition is not an issue for them, nor is that down payment on a first house. Students like mine sit back in their chairs and dare you to shake them out of their complacency. This attitude is so pervasive that the faculty have nicknamed Fairview "Laissez Faire," which somehow became "Lazy Fair." When I contrast Fairview with King High School, where I did my student teaching . . . well, the point is, I accepted a job *here*. No one twisted my arm.

When I got home after school that day, the phone was ringing. I ran to get it, dropping my bag of groceries in the process. Big mistake. It was Sara.

"I just heard the news."

"What news?"

"Now don't be coy with me, Mike."

No one was ever coy with Sara. "What do you want, Sara?"

"Is that any way to talk to your wife?"

"You're not my wife." As I talked I lifted an empty Coke can off a chair so I could sit down.

"Ah, what a difference a year makes."

"What a difference your moving in with Buddy made." I tried my luck shooting the empty can across the room into the waste bin. I missed it. It would have been a three-point play had it gone in, but alas, it took its place beside my other failures. Basketball was never my sport.

"Now, now. That's old news."

"Does that mean you're dumping Buddy?"

Sara laughed. It was part of her repertoire. "You're trying to change the subject, Mike."

"And what subject is that?"

"Your newly acquired wealth."

"What happened? Did it get published on the front page of the *Post* or something?"

"I know you would like to have kept it quiet."

"What do you want, Sara?"

"For myself? Nothing. For the children . . . you know I have to look out for their welfare."

"Your children. Not mine. By your first marriage, remember? Why don't you call Lance if you need some more dough? I'm already sending you monthly checks."

The laugh was turned on again. "Let's be serious, Mike. You know your payments were fixed upon the assumption of your having a teacher's salary."

"Which is lower than your salary at the Treasury Department and a fraction of Buddy's bucks as a so-called real estate developer."

"We're going backward again."

"No. *You* are. If you'd had the decency to marry Buddy, I'd be off the hook for supporting Lance's kids. This whole set-up stinks, and if you think –"

"It's not what *I* think that matters, Mike. It's what the court thinks. Now, if you want to go back to court . . ."

"Good-bye, Sara."

"Not so fast –"

Click. Sara was gone.

I disconnected the phone and then set about picking the groceries up off the floor. In theory, my postage-stamp one-bedroom makes straightening up a breeze. I was almost done when Mookie walked in.

"Yo, man."

Startled, I knocked over the bag of groceries again with my knee. Mookie smiled. He had an infectious smile that made his smooth, olive, Vietnamese skin seem to glow. For a moment he stood there watching me scramble about on all fours.

"What are you doing down on the floor?" he asked.

"Searching for my long-lost aunt."

Mookie followed me into the kitchenette carrying an apple I'd failed to retrieve. He rubbed it once on the side of his face and began chomping away.

"Want some dinner, Mookie?"

"Dinner? No. I ate lunch. No time for dinner. Besides, I need a favor."

What? Not Mookie, too. As a neighbor in my building, he was totally outside the network of my friends and acquaintances. How had he found out about my inheritance?

"What's the favor?"

"I need some wheels."

"You want to borrow my car?"

"Yeah. My engine's busted up. I got to get to Rosecroft for the races tonight."

"Your new sports car's busted, so you want to borrow my old Pontiac?"

"Hey, man, a Celica isn't exactly a sports car."

I was thinking about the way Mookie drove cars. Fast.

". . . and it isn't new, either."

"Oh, I'm sorry," I replied. "What is it then, a year old?"

"Two years. Almost. It'll be two years in August."

I looked down, screwed up my face, and slowly shook my head. Then I turned to Mookie and smiled, "In August? You bought your car in August? Who buys a car in August?"

"Well, what do ya say?"

"The keys are on the floor over there. Next to my book bag and errant three-pointer." I hadn't had a chance to pick them up after my sprint to the phone.

Mookie pushed his thin lips out and nodded his head as he jive-walked over to the keys. He reached his arms down in an exaggerated dance move and lifted them up with two fingers. Then he swiveled and jived back. He left the Coke can where it was.

"What are you auditioning for?" I laughed.

"Hey, what's the problem? I'm half American, remember? An Amerasian with *soul*."

I shook my head and began putting away the perishables. When I turned around again, Mookie was still there, combing his stringy black hair with one hand and swinging my keys like a pendulum with the other.

"What's the matter? I said you could take it. Just don't wreck it, that's all. I can't afford to replace it."

A pained expression drew itself across Mookie's face. We stood in silence as I watched him grimace. "Um, there's just one little problem . . . you see . . ." He sidled around my tiny counter and jangled the keys close to his face. "It's about my license."

"You lost your driver's license?"

"Just a technicality. I'll get it back in a week. But, meanwhile, I've got to get to Rosecroft tonight. Can you take me?"

"What's so important about tonight?"

"I've got the winners."

"Sure, Mookie."

"It's the truth. I swear by the Holy Virgin."

"I thought you were Buddhist."

"Amerasian, remember? I can be any combination I want to be."

"This is bullshit, Mookie."

"No, I've got to go. I owe some money. I know the winners."

"If you owe some money, the track's the last place to be. Look, if you're short, I'll lend you some –"

Now it was Mookie's turn to laugh. "Look, I may be cashed out, but at least I've got my principles."

I was thankful someone did, so I drove Mookie over to the track.

When we got there, Mookie was very insistent that we sit in a particular section. Then he took a racing form from his hip pocket. He was betting on four races. He went into long explanations about why certain horses and riders were better than others.

A race was already in progress as we settled in. The lights were on but it wasn't fully dark yet. The October air was brisk and refreshing. The crowd was a strange mixture. I'd never been to horse races before. The whole idea of horses racing against each other seemed rather unusual to me. This was because horses were no longer the normal form of transportation. However, as an historian I could picture it as a throwback to the horse-and-buggy days – or perhaps to the days of ancient Rome and the charioteers. I preferred this way of thinking about it.

"So this is what you do when you place the bets," Mookie began.

A sharp knee in the back ended my vision. "I'm not betting," I said as I turned to see the culprit. An old woman was seated behind me scanning her racing form like a veteran. Her shoulder-length gray hair and brightly colored clothes lent her an air of aggressive eccentricity. I turned back around without saying anything.

"No, you don't understand," Mookie said. "I want you to place my bets."

I screwed up my face. Mookie motioned for me to lean closer. He spoke in very subdued tones. "You see, I got this inside information. Tip. That's what I got. A tip. And you see, I can't bet it."

"You can't bet a tip?" I asked a little too loudly. He motioned for me to be quieter.

"They got rules and regulations. Very strict. Look. I'm desperate. Very important. All you got to do is bet the races I've got circled on the form. I've got all the money. Here." He furtively thrust a wad of bills into my hand and pushed me out of my seat and in the direction of the betting windows. "I wrote it all out. No problem."

As I walked over to the windows, it occurred to me that the real reason Mookie wanted me to take him to the track was so that I could place his bets. That driver's license story was probably a lie. Since when did Mookie bother with such things as driver's licenses, anyway?

No. Somebody had warned Mookie to stay away from the track. But Mookie had seen a chance to get a cut for himself. Only he had to "watch out" for that *somebody*. That's where I came in.

What worried me was whether that *somebody* had been watching and was now watching *me*. A wiry old lady pushed ahead of me, digging her elbow into my ribs as she passed. It was the same old woman who had been seated behind me. I was about to say something to her when I noticed that her right arm was withered; it simply didn't work. Suddenly, her girlishly long gray hair and garish clothes no longer seemed a badge of aggressiveness. I felt guilty at having been angry at her at all. I moved in line behind her. The crowd in front of the steel-barred betting booths emanated restless anxiety. People of all shapes and sizes closely guarded their picks as they waited for their tote tickets – tickets they hoped would bring them into some money.

When it was my turn, I stepped up to the black bars. The young blond-haired man seated behind the bars might have been a bank teller. I started to tell him my bets but, not having a very good understanding of track betting, I was apparently using the wrong language. This was my first time, and the whole experience was totally foreign. So I ended up sliding my racing form under the thick protective glass to the man.

This got results.

In short order, I had a handful of tickets. I made my way back to the grandstand. When I got to my seat, I found that Mookie was not there. Nor was the old lady.

Not knowing what to do but wait, I set about trying to make sense of how betting worked. It seems that there are three basic bets: win, place, and show. The latter two pay off more often, and so they pay less money. The racing odds are always changing and are a function of the betting activity. Kind of like the stock market. My bets were all "to win." People around me were trying combination bets, with exotic names such as "exacta," "perfecta," and "daily double." Mookie had kept it simple. Less to foul up.

I was mulling this over, when the bells sounded and the race began. For the first few moments the horses maintain the line order they had at the starting gate. But just as your eyes have a fix on everything, the jockeys move their mounts in a daring cut to the inside lane as they make the first turn. This is dangerous stuff. Ten horses in a bunch doing forty or fifty miles per hour with a clearance between animals of half-a-foot. A sudden miscalculation would be a fatal mistake.

As the horses rounded the first turn, the tight conglomeration had thinned so that no more than three horses were abreast. I tried to match the racing form numbers to the modern-day charioteers. But the task was futile. I had to look up to witness the backstretch where animal muscles shined from the overhead floodlights. At this point the horses seemed to be moving in slow motion: a captivating display of power and grace. The line of racers was thin and growing longer. At the front was a horse whose jockey was wearing blue. Behind him, by the length of a horse, was a rider in red.

When they entered the last turn it seemed like blue had it wrapped. But coming out of the turn, red swung wide and was pulling up. Blue didn't like this and I thought I saw the jockey swing his stick at the other rider. I didn't think that seemed legal.

Blue was flogging his horse but to no avail. Red had pulled even when suddenly it was over. Who had won?

I looked up to the scoreboard. The results were displayed so that even a neophyte like me could follow them. I looked at the winner, then at the tickets in my hand. Mookie's horse had won. With the urging of some people around me, I went back to the betting windows to collect Mookie's winnings. I learned the routine after a couple of races. After three of Mookie's picks came through, I stopped returning to my seat with my winnings. I was getting too many winners. I didn't want to draw attention.

Instead, I hung out in the indoor lounge, where they filled your glass and dulled your mind to everything except the closed-circuit television image of what was happening outside on the track. It seemed incredible to me that people would watch a race on a screen when they could be seeing it firsthand. But perhaps

I was missing the whole point of it all. The cosmic lotto: betting. A way to beat one's karma. Watching the people sitting there under a smoky cloud from their cigarettes made me want to drink. I decided it was time to step outside.

"It's all in the stars," said a young man in a brown, well-worn suit, who was standing just outside the lounge.

"The stars?"

"Yeah. You gotta believe."

"The stars?"

"The zodiac controls us all. Let me know your sign and we can sit down together."

I turned away and heard a priest explaining to an open-mouthed, jug-eared man, "Do you think they name these horses randomly? What you do is assign a value to each letter. *A* gets one, and *B* gets two, and so forth. Then you add them all up and divide by the day of the year . . ."

I walked on.

A woman in what looked to be a turban was explaining her system to anyone who would listen. "What you do is throw out the red herrings. They always put a few in the race to trick you. Once you've gotten rid of the red herrings . . ."

Young women. Young men. Clergymen. Clergywomen. Stockbrokers. Plumbers. Fishmongers. "Soldier, scholar, horse-man, he / And all he did done perfectly / As though he had but that one trade alone."

I wonder if Yeats bet on horses. He *was* Irish.

I found myself returning to the lounge and watching the next couple of races with a Jameson in one hand and Mookie's racing form in the other.

There goes my budget. It was true. My budget was too tight for five-dollar drinks at the track. Of course I had a million dollars, but at this point all that was play money. I didn't really believe in it anyway.

I drank my money. My pockets were stuffed with cash. But, unfortunately, it belonged to Mookie.

After the last race I was broke, my own money spent on drinks. Tomorrow – later this morning – I'd have to face the five-thirty alarm and early-morning cross-country practice. Right now, I wanted to find Mookie and give him his money.

My head was spinning. Whiskey has a way of sneaking up on you. Just when you think you're safe, it shows up.

I collected myself and headed toward the car. I'm always forgetting where I've parked and often have this dark fantasy of wandering endlessly in a gigantic parking lot never to find my way out. "Man found dead in row 444E. Keys still in hand."

As I descended the stadium's cement ramps, I saw the old woman with the lame arm. In any other circumstance, she would have been an object of pity – but now she brought me out of my daze. Perhaps it was my imagination, but I thought she was watching me.

I started bumping into people.

"Qué pasa, compadre?"

I looked around and saw Mookie. "Since when do you speak Spanish, Mookie?"

"Since when do I do anything, compadre?"

We drove home on the freeway. I was watching out for my turn. It was a turn-off that I often missed because the exit sign was not for an exit. It led to another freeway – the Beltway. An exit takes you off a freeway and not onto another one. Anyway, I remembered the wad of bills in my pocket.

"Seventy-three hundred. Nice job," said Mookie after he counted out the money while we were still seated in my car in the apartment parking lot. "How much do you want, Michael?"

I waved my hand in the air. I didn't want his profits. Mookie didn't press the point. He scrambled out. "Hey man, I *owe* you."

I lingered in my car, thinking about the old woman with the withered arm. I wondered, suddenly, if she had played any role in Mookie's winnings, and if I'd ever see her again. Then I heard a car engine start. I watched Mookie drive away in his Celica.

It was time to go to bed.

Once in my apartment, I saw that I had never picked up my backpack from where I'd dropped it earlier. I knelt down. Next to it was my mail: an advertisement from Macy's, some shampoo samples, and a letter from Ash. How could I have missed it?

Chapter Two

12 St Georges Avenue
London, N7
October 21, 1990

Dear Michael,

I've found an apartment in a quaint section of London known as Tufnell Park.

I live on the middle story of a house run by an Irish landlady, Mrs Flanagan. (Imagine her surprise when she discovered my name was Aisling!) I have two rooms – a rather large bedroom and a kitchen – that are not connected; the stairwell runs between them. I share a bathroom with a New Zealand couple upstairs, who seem very nice except that the man plays rock and roll on an electric guitar each night from 9 to 11. He accompanies a tape that has his favorite songs sans lead guitar.

I've also moved into my study carrel at the University of London, and have met my contact person, Dr Hugh Selwyn Mauberley. Amazingly, he looks a lot like *you*, except that he's about ten years older, a couple of inches shorter, and sports a tightly cropped beard. I look forward to our work together on Donne.

The city is everything I hoped it would be – and more. Let me tell you a story to illustrate my point. As you know, before I left for London, I sent myself a box of working materials. When I went out to Heathrow to pick them up, I got lost. You see, the air cargo building is not located near the regular passenger terminal. I had to walk a very long way. I arrived just at closing time and picked up my parcel. Fine. I had my box, but what was I to do with it? It was too far to walk back to the terminal with a heavy box, and since they'd just closed the air cargo office, I couldn't call a taxi. I was in a fix. Then a man who worked in maintenance (John was his name) pulled up in his car. I asked him if he could drive me to the main passenger building. Well, not only could he help me, but he drove me all the way into central London. "You can't manage on the Underground with a box like that," he said.

Can you believe it? He wouldn't even accept reimbursement for his gas. Even dropped me off at the hotel I was staying at before I found my flat. I was bowled over.

England is just so different from America. I wouldn't think of trusting someone like that in the United States. I just know this is going to be a great year. Hope your classes are going fine. Are you coaching cross-country again?

Love,
Aisling

I put the letter down. It had been a long day. I didn't want to reread any of it. I had to get up at five thirty.

During the night, I dreamed I was in the alcove of my church with Father McGinnis, waiting for Aisling to walk down the aisle. It was the day we were to be married. Time in the dream was measured by the cigarettes Father McGinnis was smoking. One. Two. Three. Four. The ash on the fifth one was curling inward. I stared hard at it. It looked so solid. I clung to that image, hoping everything would stay the same. But of course that was an illusion. I knew that one strong puff of air and the ash would dissipate into nothingness.

Autumn mornings foretell the chilling that is about to come. It was cold at six thirty. Ten boys dressed in maroon sweats went out in three groups from the back door of the locker room. Mornings: the purpose was "easy over distance." Increase endurance. It's not possible to work high school boys too hard. They can take almost anything.

They took off, dead-eyed. The puffs of condensation from their breath marked their progress until they were out of sight. On my clipboard I had their groups and times recorded. In cross-country we record everything.

I walked back into the locker room and poured myself a large mug of coffee. The place was a mess. I set down my mug and picked up about forty towels that had missed the huge bin in the corner. "Good thing they aren't trying out for basketball," I said out loud to no one.

My boys dressed near to the door. They would be running for miles, but wanted to save a few feet of locker room space. I kicked some of their street shoes under the long wooden benches so they wouldn't trip when they got back. Boys have a tendency to space out after morning runs. One of the shoes hit a metal support post under the bench and bounced out again.

Soccer wasn't my game, either.

I picked up my coffee again and took in the aroma of my coffee with that of generations of sweat, soaked into the very concrete blocks that had been painted over and over and over again with thick layers of white paint. Of course I was happy that Ash was enjoying London. She had wanted to go there all her life, and now she had a chance to work with a top name on her still-uncompleted dissertation. But she seemed so far away.

Then I thought about the old lady and Bernie. I don't know why I pictured them together.

"Hi, stranger."

I looked up. It was Angie.

"The men's locker room? This is a bit brave even for you, isn't it?"

"Michael, you're such a tease." She came over and sat next to me on the long wooden bench. "I thought I'd at least find you in the shower."

"What do you want, Angie?"

She smiled and cleared her throat. "I need you."

"Oh?"

"For a project," she quickly added. "Shakespearean England. The history behind the history plays and all that. I thought you might be able to help me. It wouldn't take too much time. You see, we're having a special event. It'll last the whole morning. I'm really excited about it."

Somehow it was hard for me to imagine Angie having genuine enthusiasm for serious academic pursuits. Maybe I'd judged her too harshly.

"We need someone to go over the Wars of the Roses and a few other tidbits. The whole thing will be in dress-up, of course."

I looked at her. She was really rather attractive in her way. Blonde, northern Italian. Brown almond-shaped eyes. Buxom, yet not heavy. She was a head shorter than I was. Surname Santini. "The Wars of the Roses, huh? Tell me more."

"No time just now. Are you free after school?"

"I have cross-country practice."

"When is that done?"

"Five or so."

"We could take a sandwich at Schwartz's Deli."

I thought for a moment. What would involve less time: a sandwich at a deli or an evening in my apartment. "That sounds fine. I'll meet you there at five fifteen."

"Don't be late; you know they stop serving sandwiches at six."

Six sounded fine, but before I could respond, I heard a slamming on the outer locker room door. The harriers were back. The reckoning time was at hand.

One of my big weakness has always been staying in my empty classroom during break periods. The standard procedure is to trot off to the faculty lounge for coffee and discussion while grading papers. Sometimes I went there, but usually I hunkered down behind my desk while students trickled in to unburden their hearts and souls.

I had finished only a paragraph of the research paper I was reading when I was interrupted.

"Mr O'Meara?"

I looked up, recognizing the face but not the name of one of my senior girls. I smiled. She was chewing gum at a furious pace.

"Are you busy?"

"No, have a seat." What was I supposed to say? "I only spend my time dithering away like this in the hope that one of you will come in and give my life meaning"?

"I'm trying to decide which college to apply to and I thought you might be able to help."

Everyone at Fairview will go to college – somewhere.

"How far along are you in your thinking?"

"I don't know. My father made a list for me. But I'm not so sure." The gum popped. She didn't miss a beat as she brushed her bangs out of her eyes. It was a futile gesture.

"Do you have the list?"

She handed me a ball of paper from the recesses of her purse and sat down at a nearby desk.

I flattened the list and read: Princeton, Yale, University of Maryland, and St Angeline's. "Well, this runs the gamut. Where's St Angeline's?"

"You've never heard of it? No one's ever heard of it. Actually, I think the school sucks."

I shrugged and handed her back the list.

"What I really want is to go local and hang out at Georgetown. A lot of rich guys go there."

"Oh really?"

"Oh yeah. I want to marry a rich Georgetown law student."

"You want to go to college just to marry a rich boy?"

"Oh, I won't stay married to him. Oh no. I'm too smart for that. I'll divorce him and take half of his money."

I thought of Sara.

The girl was now on the edge of her seat. This was serious business. "No. Half is *too good* for him. To have *me* it's going to *cost* him. I want more than half. I want . . ." She struggled for an appropriate number. "*A third!* Yeah, that's right. He's not going to get away without giving me at least a third!"

Fortunately, I was saved by the bell.

During the afternoon cross-country practice I began to think about the million dollars again. I know this is going to sound strange, but I had had time to think about it and I was beginning to have second thoughts about the whole thing. After all, I had been getting on fine without the money. I had a job in which I felt I was doing some good. I had a quasi-fiancée (a promise without a date). And how many other people have the time or the inclination to read the great thinkers of history and discuss them with people?

My life wasn't so bad.

On the other hand, teaching is a burn-out job when you do it *right*. And for what? The gum-chewing student whose sole pre-occupation is keeping her hair out of her eyes and finding a husband? Did I *really* want to spend my spirit on these pampered offspring of privilege? Still, public school students – even in areas of wealth – were little better than private school kids. The spoiled kids at Fairview had a lot in common with the students I'd taught at King High School in Boston: fatherless families, drug and alcohol abuse, and an ethos centered around the acquisition of *things*. It was the same in both environments. *Things* made every-thing all right for them.

Maybe these kids needed me. It was all a jumble in my mind. And what would money do to resolve this jumble? When I first learned of the inheritance, it was all I could think about. I tried to imagine the sum from different perspectives. I could take a lump sum and live it up. I could take my twenty-five-thousand-dollar-a-year salary for forty years, and I'd be dead before it ran out. Or I could give stipends to the various people who'd been important to me. But many of these people were already dead.

"What'd I get, coach?"

A student's voice broke me out of my reverie. I'd missed the kid's time but quickly guesstimated from my watch. "Two-sixteen." Now the rest of the boys were finishing. I read off their times to them as they crossed the finish line: "Two-thirty-nine! Two-forty! Forty-one, two, three . . ."

Then I began timing the rest period. Two-minute rest. Then another half-mile interval. Speed work. Hell on wheels.

"All right!" I yelled. That meant thirty seconds. Everything recorded. Recorded and put into a book. It's always important that it be in a book – somewhere.

"Excuse me, Mr O'Meara?"

I was leaving the locker room on my way to my appointment with Angie at Schwartz's deli when I found myself confronted by a short, stocky man dressed in a dark suit and sunglasses. His head looked like a rectangular block of weathered wood balanced upon his sawhorse shoulders.

"Do you mind if I have a word with you?" The man flashed a badge for a nanosecond then put it in his jacket pocket. I shrugged my shoulders, wondering if any of my runners were still around.

"I have a couple of questions for you," the man said. He grabbed me roughly by the elbow and guided me over to a bench where he told me to sit down.

I preferred standing. "Are you a cop?"

"No. I'm an investigator for the racetrack."

"The racetrack? What kind of investigator?"

"Look, Mr O'Meara, it's my job to follow-up on *unusual* events."

"Like two-headed babies and spaceships from Mars?"

The man straightened his lapel. *Nice clothes*, I thought.

"No. It's more like a man who comes out of nowhere and wins seven thousand dollars at the track."

I couldn't believe it. This was about last night, my evening at the track with Mookie – or, rather, without Mookie. I cleared my throat, beginning to feel nervous. "Surely that's not so unusual," I said.

The man's expression didn't change. I saw myself reflected in his sunglasses. "Had you been to Rosecroft before last night?"

"What business is it of yours? And how is it that you're tracking people down? What did you do – run my license plate number? There has to be a law against that sort of thing."

"It's my business to protect the integrity of horse racing in this state. Let's just say that there were several 'red flags' in your case."

"What are you, anyway? You don't work for the state. They're not that efficient. Besides, your suit costs too much. Hey, I'd love to chat but I'm late for an appointment."

I moved to go. The man stepped in front of me. He didn't touch me, but his movement was threatening.

"It's in your best interest to cooperate, Mr O'Meara – *if* you're really innocent." Then he turned and walked away.

I turned in the direction of Schwartz's Deli, but grew angrier with every step. I turned back around to yell something at the man, but he had vanished. All that was there was the quiet opulence of Laissez Faire.

"I'd almost given up on you," Angie began when I arrived at the deli. Schwartz's Deli was a combination bakery, sandwich shop, and bar. In the daytime the front part (near the ceiling-to-floor-length windows) was where the customers gathered. From five o'clock on, the movement was toward the booths in the back as the clientele transitioned as well. Angie was seated in a booth. In front of her was a half-empty glass of beer next to an empty one whose foam was sliding down the sides. "I've got a lot to give you."

I took a seat thinking about Mookie. I decided that he was up to something bad.

"You've got to order," Angie said.

"What's good?" That man hadn't been a cop or a state investigator. His badge was probably a phony. Why would Mookie have set me up? I had thought I was a good judge of character. Then I remembered my marriage to Sara.

Finally, I looked at whom I was eating with. "I'll take that," I said in response to a recommendation from Angie, without hearing what she had recommended. I hadn't even picked up a menu. Angie took charge on the drinks order, too, and soon I was sipping some tasteless beer.

"It's called Alexander Hamilton," she said. "It's produced by a microbrewery in West Virginia, where they have an ancient Indian spring that gives it a unique, grainy quality."

"Probably coal tailings," I said uncharitably.

"It won a national prize," Angie continued without missing a beat. "I read about it in . . ."

It still tasted like coal water.

Our meals came. I had the corned beef sandwich (their specialty). It was a sandwich that stood four inches high! No one could fit it into his mouth at one time so I took it as a challenge. They gave you a pickle on the side with some chips so that you could munch on them while you figured out your strategy before you attempted the feat.

Angie had the chicken noodle soup that came with four slices of garlic bread. At first, Angie didn't touch her food. "Michael, how are you going to eat that?" She giggled and I smiled, reflexively.

"The point of a deli sandwich is not to question why, but to do or – choke on it, I suppose." We both laughed at that lame attempt at witticism.

Angie almost took a piece of garlic bread to dip into her soup, but then stopped and leaned forward on the table and put her chin on her hands. "I'm going to watch this."

And then I did what anyone else has done who's eaten at a deli-restaurant-bar that gives you such a challenge, I triangulated the problem and began at the bottom and aimed at the middle. This gave a massive bite that was followed by a companion strategy (top to middle at the complementary angle).

These two bites elicited commendation from my dinner companion. "Well done, Michael. It almost makes me want to exchange my soup for your sandwich so I can give it a go."

I bowed my head in appreciation.

Angie then took her first bite: she dipped a morsel of bread into her soup and bit off half of that – perhaps a quarter of an inch. She looked up as if I should give her applause. But I demurred.

"So are you interested in the *money* – excuse me, I mean the Shakespeare project?"

"You know me, Angie. I love history. I guess that means you can count me in – unless I have to do too much."

Angie laughed. "That's what everyone says. I'm happy to go on board so long as you, dear Angie, do all the work. What's the problem? Do I have the sign 'sucker' pasted to my backside?"

I took another giant bite of corned beef.

Angie held her pose momentarily, but then couldn't stay still-framed forever so she decided to take her own sampling of dinner via the conventional soupspoon. I watched her carefully. She pushed in the spoon in a semicircular motion beginning away from her then descending into the broth and reascending directly to her mouth from which she consumed the portion in whole. I was instantly reminded of Asling who dipped her soupspoon in the other way (i.e., beginning at close proximity and moving away from the self and then consuming the portion on a gradual reverse dipping motion).

"You're nobody's fool, Angie," I said. "I just don't want to over-commit."

"Ah, commitment. The twentieth-century male phobia."

I took another giant bite.

We continued in this way with Angie coyly approaching her food and then pressing me on the Shakespeare project. I finally agreed to do some research on the Wars of the Roses to back up the Henry plays. When I was successfully recruited, she immediately ate two whole pieces of garlic bread, a couple of spoonfuls of soup, and drank the rest of the half-empty beer.

Then we went through the back-and-forth of splitting the check. Angie put her hand on top of mine, "I suppose it won't be long before you'll be picking up all of the checks." She giggled again. I tried to paste on a smile. Then, somehow Angie's hand had ended up on my knee, so that when I rose to go she was left clutching my napkin that she held in the air like a limp flag.

At the apartment building, I tried everything: the door, the bell, the fire escape, even the kitchen window. No Mookie.

I wrote him a note and slid it under his door. He would come by if he had any sense of decency. This gave me a small sense of satisfaction. Very small.

When I returned to my apartment my phone was ringing. Against my better judgment I answered it. Big mistake.

Chapter Three

"Mike, I've fixed you."

"Bernie?"

"Well, it's not Jimmy Hoffa."

"I thought you were coming by tomorrow."

"No time. Got a break. Got to move. Life waits for no man, you know."

"Right, Bernie."

"I'll be by in thirty. Be outside. I don't like to wait."

Then there was dial tone.

That's the way it was with Bernie. When we were in college he was "vanguard antiwar" and all that. A man of his time. "You're too conservative, Mike," he used to tell me. "Not *in touch*. You've got to be in touch."

Bernie was in touch – but with *what*? I was never quite sure. One thing I was sure of was that he was a mover and a shaker while I was more "the shaken." I needed Bernie.

He was there in twenty. At seven thirty. I was sitting on the stoop in the cool October air, watching the cars pull up: commuters home from work. Newly minted yuppies in their expensive cars living in my no-nothing building. But the building had a Bethesda zip code, and they had their fancy cars. What else did they need – except the real thing? Which they'd get soon enough. First, they'd graduate to a condo, and then to a home in Potomac or McLean. It was part of their preordained career path.

"Mike, I've fixed you," Bernie said as he stepped out of his currency-green Mercedes.

"How's that, Bernie?"

Bernie walked up to my car, parked in front of my door, and put his foot on the aging, rusting bumper, which I'd reattached myself, with bolts purchased from the hardware store. I stared at Bernie's foot wondering if my work would hold.

"We can't talk here," Bernie said. "Let's go to my club."

"Your *club*?"

"Damn right." He kicked the bumper so that it shook, then walked back to his Mercedes.

I followed (pausing only to see if the bolts were still firmly in place).

"Look, old salt, the time's past when you have to worry about that dilapidated jalopy."

I didn't reply. I got in the passenger side of his car and, heeding the car's electronic chimes, fastened my seat belt. We drove down Massachusetts Avenue, to the Jockey Club, an elegant, old red-brick building that fit into the environment of "Embassy Row." A valet parked Bernie's car, and we went inside.

"Here, put this on," Bernie said, handing me a tie from a rack in the cloakroom. "Even in the bar you've got to wear a tie, old salt."

I stared at the gray-and-red slanted stripes. "This doesn't go, Bernie," I said, staring at the tie.

"Of course it does; I've got an eye for that," he replied, taking matters into his own hand and tightening the noose around my neck.

I hadn't been thinking about the colors.

In the bar, we took seats in high-backed, studded leather chairs that seemed to surround us. With the chairs enveloping us as they were, it felt almost as if we were seated in a private conference room.

Bernie ordered Rob Roys and opened up a file folder between us on the dark textured table. From the pile of papers, which Bernie had clipped in some esoteric order, he produced a check and handed it to me.

"There you are, Mike, one million dollars."

I gazed at the check. It had to be good if it were drawn from Chase Manhattan, I thought, while saying out loud, "A lot of zeros there." I must have gazed at it for quite a while because when the waiter came with the drinks (probably five minutes or so) I felt that only a second had passed.

"Damn right, a lot of zeros."

The waiter came back with our drinks and set them down on coasters. Bernie watched him do so. I stared down at the check, holding it so that the waiter couldn't see it. Mechanically, I grouped the zeros by threes to verify the number. One million. There seemed to be no mistake. When the waiter had walked away, I looked up at Bernie and said, "That's one expensive piece of paper."

"One piece of coded paper with magnetic threads, watermarks, and special opaque inks that cannot be photocopied," Bernie corrected.

"My life is to be changed by one piece of paper."

Bernie laughed and downed his Rob Roy while signaling to the waiter for another. "It'll take more than that to change your life, Mike. But don't lose the moment. Touch it. Caress it. Kiss it. Just don't *eat* it."

I set the check down on the table next to my untouched drink. A moment later, the waiter came back, and then the check sat between *two* untouched drinks. Kind of a bridge.

When the waiter was gone, Bernie said, "I'd like to let you stare at it all night, old salt, but we've got work to do. Drink up. You can't do business on an empty stomach."

I put my hand to my glass. It was squat and sturdy and held a lot of liquid. It would probably have held a whole can of Coke, or more. It wasn't easy to hold the glass in my small hands. I wanted to wait, but the glass was already to my lips.

"Now I'm going to give you a crash course in 'Investing According to Bernie.' Listen closely because we've a lot to go through in a short time."

Bernie talked. I drank.

He told me that inflation and the government were my worst enemies and that I needed to be "aggressive" if I wanted my money to grow so that I might become "really rich." He would separate my money into funds that had investment "objectives" and were all coordinated to quadruple the total in ten years.

"I don't know, Bernie. Don't high-yield investments have high risks?"

"You reap what you sow, old salt. Put your money in a hole and it will rot on you. You've got to 'use it or lose it.'" Bernie had a lot of phrases like that.

I was finding it hard to concentrate on the matter at hand. There was so much to consider, so much I didn't understand. Various papers were put before me to sign and then yanked away. Finally, after he had finished with the show, Bernie said, "One more thing . . . I'd put it off, but we've got to do it tonight."

"Look, Bernie, I'm tired – ." I put down my glass, which always seemed to be full.

"Look, old salt, the companies were slow on their end and then there are additional taxes, penalties, and everything if we sit on this. Time waits for no man."

Bernie shoved a paper in front of me that read, "Power of Attorney." With a smile, he handed me his Mont Blanc pen. "Take your time and sign."

"What does this mean, Bernie?"

"Just a formality in order for me to handle your finances."

My head was spinning. "I don't know, Bernie. This seems a bit extreme."

"Don't you trust me? If you don't trust me, we can end this right now."

"No, Bernie, it's not that. But I do like to retain *control*."

"Listen, don't let the words fool you. This is a limited power of attorney that is revocable anytime you say."

I looked at the paper again. "Where does it say that, Bernie?"

"Well, it doesn't in so many words. But the intent is clear."

"Humor me, Bernie. Let's write the words in."

"You might invalidate a legal contract – " Bernie started to say, but I was already writing. It never occurred to me that my scribbling might be meaningless. Instead, I turned my attention to one other detail: the banker's fund (that is, the money that would be at my disposal, and not tied up in investments). "I think we need a little more in here, Bernie."

Bernie sighed heavily. "Look, do you want me to handle this or not? You know I wouldn't be doing this if we hadn't gone to school together. I mean the college tie and all that."

I leaned toward him. "Two hundred-fifty thousand in that fund would let me quit working at the hardware store."

"Mike. It pays only six percent."

"But that's fifteen thousand a year. My bills would be clear."

"Do you know what that would do to the goals I've set for you?"

"Bernie."

"You don't want to do this, Mike."

"I want to do it, Bernie. The most I'll allow in the high risk category is four hundred thousand."

My head was spinning for the second night in a row as I rode home in a taxi that Bernie had paid for. He'd been angry that he wasn't controlling every cent. He'd said I didn't trust him. Said he'd just as soon forget the whole thing. But in the end, he came around. Two hundred-fifty thousand went into the bankers' fund, which was as safe as the bank itself. Another three hundred-fifty thousand went into a money market fund with the very same bank with a minimum deposit period of one year, while four hundred thousand would be split among various pools of progressively "higher-growth" vehicles (read: riskier investments).

This was what they called "putting a portfolio together."

According to Bernie, in ten years I'd be able to back away from my "growth" objective and slide into "income" as an objective. Then I could retire to the "south of France" (as Bernie said over and over).

What would it be like never to sweat the bills again? Never to have to send a check out for which I didn't have the funds? No more night jobs at the hardware store. No more financial worries – ever!

The prospect seemed really attractive. For this I could put up with Bernie and his 1 percent commission. That night, I crawled into bed and fell asleep dreaming about taking up golf and horseback riding.

The next morning, Wednesday, I awoke to the radiant beauty of an Indian summer. We'd had a frost the week before, but now a warm glow reigned – at least for today.

And I was determined to be sanguine.

At school, one of my runners strained a hamstring, and I comforted and lectured him concurrently on stretching and fate. Angie waylaid me twice. "We really need a full planning session on when your Wars of the Roses piece will be done and its scope. I know you're very busy but . . ."; "I guess what you want is a take-charge woman. Well, here I am. I've written out our schedule. I'll remind you when. . . ." I didn't listen to the rest of what she said.

I ambled over to the Humanities teachers' lounge and mechanically checked the message board (a huge corkboard upon which messages were tacked according to a very loose concession to the alphabet). It was then that I discovered that Sara had left three cryptically threatening messages for me. And my injured runner hobbled in during my break period and unburdened himself to me.

I decided to treat myself to a book. Bethesda has several secondhand bookstores, but I generally went to the one a few blocks from school, next to the deli where Angie and I had our meeting.

The warmth of the day was lingering, and the old books smelled musty. My general policy about books was never to buy one unless I felt distinctly compelled to do so. Otherwise, I'd have been broke. Broker. But now, I guess . . . well, it's hard to break old habits.

The books were arranged two deep on the shelves. This meant that you had to pull out the front book in order to get a look at the one behind it. The hidden books were often better, since most people never bothered or knew to look back there.

I unconsciously thumbed through an old edition of Donne's *Songs and Sonnets*. I fancy poetry a little, but facts were more my game. I decided to move on to the History and Classics sections. I came upon a clean copy of Euclid's *Elements*, edited by Heath with a commentary by Mueller. I snatched it up.

One book was generally my limit, but by the time I got to the register I had managed to pick up another. It was volume one of Lord Macaulay's *History of England*. It was a beautifully bound book in light brown calfskin with a seven-rib-spine and a gold-leaf imprint of the seal of the Order of the Garter on the cover with the motto: *honi soit qui mal y pense*. It was in excellent condition with most of the gilt still left on the pages. The end papers were clean and not tattered. Macaulay would also be useful for my project with Angie since his conservative political mindset is sympathetic with Shakespeare's. I leafed through the first chapter and came upon these words, "The events which I propose to relate form only a single act of a great and eventful drama extending through ages, and must be very imperfectly understood unless the plot of the preceding acts be well known."

This would take all my pocket money, but I didn't care. I *had* money. Why should I be frugal any longer? I didn't *have* to make the kinds of sacrifices I'd always made. Not any longer.

When I got home I paused before entering and stared up at my apartment building. It was an ugly brown-brick affair with dirty windows and ivy climbing the walls. Ivy may be attractive in northern climes, but in DC it means bugs. This was, after all, the South, and in the South the insect population was exponentially larger than it was in Boston.

I wondered how long I'd continue to live in this dump. Sara lived in a big Potomac house with Buddy. Would I move into that circle? I couldn't see it. No, Bethesda or maybe northwest DC was more my style. Maybe I should drive around Chevy Chase and have a look around.

It seemed like a good idea. I didn't want to go home just yet.

I revved up the Pontiac, pushed in the clutch (which made a short popping sound), and drove south on Wisconsin. When I approached the Galleria shopping mall I impulsively decided to make a short stop. I'd been inside it only once (to a specialty chocolate shop for Aisling). But now it was drawing me. I had no cash but I did have two hundred left on my credit card. Why not spend a little?

Inside the Galleria, you can feel the presence of money. Any developer can put up silver and glass, but not everyone has money behind it. But the Galleria does. Big money. I watched the women with their shopping bags. Beautiful bags with designer insignias, so shiny they looked like wrapping paper. There were few children. (I guess Galleria shopping was too serious a business for women to bring their children along.)

I wandered over to a men's store and randomly stopped at a watch display. Nobody offered to help me. I leaned over the display with utter detachment, leaving my smudgy fingerprints all over the glass. Soon a man whose collar seemed too tight asked me, in what sounded like a phony European accent, if I wanted something. I restrained my laughter as the glitter of the gold and platinum within the case suddenly revealed itself to me. They were more than timepieces. They were more than art objects.

"Show me that one," I said pointing to a thin gold-colored watch.

The man efficiently took the watch out of the case but seemed reluctant to let me touch it. It remained in his hand. There was an aura about the jewelry.

"Nice watch," I said reaching over to touch the watch. "How much?"

The man seemed offended by the question. Without looking at the price, he said, "Around twenty-two hundred."

That snapped me out of my trance. Twenty-two hundred for a watch! Give me a break. I wanted to tell the man that it was sickening for a watch to cost so much. Why, you could buy a used car for that sum. Instead, I said, "Where are the watches that are on sale?"

This really upset my want-to-be aristocrat salesperson. His eyes grew bigger as he said, "Watches in this store are *never* 'on sale.'"

Who was he trying to fool? That accent. If he were as rich as his phony accent and haughty demeanor were suggesting, then he wouldn't be working as a clerk in a retail store. "No 'sales,' eh? That's odd. I've never heard of a store that doesn't have sales."

"Then obviously you've never shopped *here* before." The man was locking up the case and turning away.

I couldn't stand it. "Wait a minute," I said, but he had already moved over to another customer, a bony, middle-aged lady dripping with gems.

For a moment I was frozen. Look, I've got plenty of money to buy a two thousand dollar watch if I wanted to. I'm a millionaire. Heck, I could buy a dozen! But what would be the point? But even as I vented mental disdain, I would not be honest if I didn't say that I did find *something* attractive about these baubles. But what was it? How strong was its force? Would it win me over, too?

I needed a change of scene so I went into a small boutique with men's suits in the window. In the store, I looked around for the racks but saw only a wall of drawers and the door to what was probably a dressing room. A young blonde woman came out.

"Can I help you?"

"Where are your suits?"

She gestured toward the drawers.

"You keep them in drawers?"

She laughed. "Oh, you mean ready-made suits. We don't carry any of *those*. We carry the material for *tailored* suits. They fit you like no others. Would you like to be measured for something?"

At least she was allowing for the possibility that I could afford to purchase something. For an instant I thought it might be pleasant to have her hands measuring me, but then thought better of it. What was I doing thinking of buying a tailored suit? I was a high school teacher. Where would I go in such a suit? "Thanks anyway."

I passed by the chocolate shop and bought a pound of chocolate for thirty dollars. And I hate chocolate. But I was determined not to leave this mall empty-handed. Besides, I needed to get my parking ticket validated. Great. Thirty dollars for parking. No wonder I'm always broke.

I walked out of the Galleria. I no longer felt like looking at houses. Instead, my thoughts were all about those watches in the case. The Cartiers and Rolexes were in a different league from the watches I was used to. *I was in a different league than what I was used to.*

Perhaps it was time for a change? But kind of change? I had to have a rich watch, but I wasn't going to spend that kind of money – even though I now had it. And yet, I couldn't put the fine jewelry watches out of my mind. Why was I obsessing on watches? I needed to do something, so I went to the automatic teller machine and drew out my balance and then some on a cash advance (19% interest).

I decided to go downtown to the Houri Palace, a little pawnshop run by an old, short, bent-over Kurdish man with a glass eye. He did a good business there just on the edge of Chinatown.

DC's Chinatown is located near the Convention Center. Consequently, there was a lot of foot traffic. People looking around. People contemplating gifts for someone back home – out of the goodness of the heart or to clear a conventioneer's bad conscience. All the same, they came to Nick's Houri Palace.

The shop window attracts the eye with Nikon cameras and expensive VCRs at prices you wouldn't believe. Inside, Nick has anything you want. And he stays open until ten.

"I've got to have a watch, Nick." Now as far as I know "Nick" is not a Kurdish name, but it's the one he uses.

"What kind of watch?"

"One that costs two hundred dollars."

"Oh, two hundred dollars," Nick said, smiling. "A nice watch I can get you for that. But why pay so much? You can buy a watch that keeps time for ten dollars."

"I want an expensive watch."

"You want a status watch."

Nick was right. His Socratic questioning forced me to clarify my muddled state of mind. "Yes. I want a status watch."

"A status watch is expensive."

"I have two hundred dollars."

"Two hundred dollars won't buy you a *real* status watch."

"Well, I have two hundred dollars."

"Look, you can buy a good watch for two hundred dollars that retails for six hundred *or* buy an imitation status watch."

"An imitation?"

"No one will know the difference."

"And you can get me one for two hundred dollars?"

"I have a selection." He took a tray from under the counter that was covered with a heavy red-velvet cloth. When Nick unveiled the treasure, I beheld a variety of watches (round, square, rectangular, of different sizes and styles propped to attention by little plastic stands anchored upon green felt).

Nick scanned the wares with his good eye and picked one for me.

"Here you are. Patek Philippe: a moon phase chronograph."

"Don't you have imitation Rolexes?"

"Too common for you. This watch here would run you twelve thousand dollars if it were real."

I was too stunned for speech. The watch looked very sleek to me. It was a round watch with a white background. The hands and casing were of gold. The hours were marked by thin roman numerals. The moon phase was just below the intersection of the hands, as were the two chronograph dials (one to each side) so that the three formed a triangle of sorts. Attached was a black watchband of soft, smooth leather.

"You see it has a stopwatch, and it's a windup watch. No batteries required: a *real watch*. Two hundred dollars is a steal."

It probably had been – stolen, I mean. I looked at Nick (hoping I had picked his good eye to stare at). "Let me try it on."

I handed Nick the money. There was never any tax at Nick's. As I left, Nick waved to me, "You look like a million dollars!"

I almost got into an accident on the way home. I was gazing at my wrist. It was hard to believe that this little watch could cost so much money. It seemed so overpriced. And yet I had to admit to a kind of fascination with the thing. *Me*, whose apartment is ersatz Second Republic (or was that Fifth Column – I was never good at math) cum Salvation Army. Aside from my books, I've never had real "nice things." *Now* knowledgeable people would think *I* was a connoisseur of time. I began to like the idea of changing my status in life. Perhaps I had finally "arrived."

When I did, I found Mookie sitting in my reading chair and watching my black-and-white portable TV.

He turned his head as I entered. "Hey, I didn't know they made sets like this anymore."

"What are you doing here? How did you get in? Did you break in?" I started toward him, but he didn't move except to pick up his Coke and take a sip. He put down the can and reached into his pocket. I was about three inches away from him and ready to throttle him.

He took out his key ring. "I've got a key."

"Where did you get that? Hand it over."

"What's the point?" he replied, finishing off the can. "Say, you don't have anything stronger than Coke around here, do you? And you should really pick up those cans over there. You keep this place like a pig sty!"

I understood: if he could make *one* key he could make *another*. There was no way to keep him out. I relaxed my clenched hands and sat down on a kitchen chair that had a chunk missing out of its black vinyl seat.

"Okay, tell me. What's this all about?"

Mookie pretended to watch the TV.

I got up and turned off Ricky Ricardo. "I said, what's this all about?"

"You know *I Love Lucy*. She's America."

"Mookie!"

He crushed the aluminum can and tossed it directly into the can: swish – a three pointer. Nothing but net. Then he turned and looked out the window. "All right. No problem. I was just minding my business when I got this tip, see. But I don't know if it's for real. So I place a few small bets and the source proved to be 'up front.' " Mookie stroked his jaw with the tips of his fingers. His smooth skin seemed to shine.

"What are you talking about?"

"A test. A trial. Understand. I can make big money."

"What does this have to do with me?"

"Look, I can see your point of view. You think that maybe I set you up or something. But I didn't. Really. The racing business is run by a bunch of gamblers, and they don't like to lose. I had to make my trial, you know, *secret*." He continued. "Hey man, there's no risk for you. They don't *know* you. You don't normally go to the track. You don't bet. So everything's cool. But *me*. I could be in real trouble if they caught me winning." Mookie averted his eyes from mine.

"What would they do to you, Mookie?"

"You don't want to know."

"Well, didn't it ever occur to you that whatever they could do to you they'd do to *me*?"

Mookie pursed his lips and waved a hand at me dismissively. "Aw, come on. You wouldn't have the money, any of it. How could they connect it to you?"

"They already have."

Mookie looked alarmed. "A small guy with a scar on his neck? A Norwegian?"

"No."

"You're lucky."

"Damn you, Mookie."

"Look, even if they were watching you, it's not like you'll start dropping money all over the place. Hey, look, I'll admit it, when you scored the other night, I knew that I was in for some bucks. I was at it myself last night. Not too big. Just enough, understand?"

"That's just great. They tie you to me, and we both get it."

"No way. The only tie to you was the other night, and . . ." Mookie hesitated.

"And what?"

"Well, I did borrow your car last night."

"You what?"

"Hey, I filled it with gas, but you see they sometimes check out the cars in the parking lot. They've got assholes on the payroll just for that."

"And I suppose your car is on their list?"

"Hey, you're getting way too jumpy. Calm down. The only way you'd be in any trouble is if you suddenly came into a lot of money. You know, started spending it big time." Mookie laughed. "That would be a stitch, wouldn't it?"

This remark was so ludicrous that Mookie stood up and steadied himself. He saw that I still didn't understand, so he added,

"Look man, you're perfectly safe. You're a struggling dude who drives an old beater car and can barely pay his bills. Am I right?"

I frowned. Mookie glanced out the window and turned back to me. He looked like a different man: hard and stern. Then in another voice he said, "Say, would you mind if I slept on your sofa tonight? It would really help me out." He sat back down on the sofa and began adjusting the cushions. He leaned over and switched off the table lamp.

What could I say?

As I made my way to the bedroom, Mookie called to me, "Hey, I really appreciate this. You've been straight. I don't forget things like that. Oh, and one more thing: You know, that Patek Philippe you've got on your wrist is a good-looking fake. I really mean it."

Chapter Four

Ten days past. I kept turning things over in my mind. And even then I was not quite sure about anything.

On the one hand, I was about to come into some money for the first time in my life. No longer would I have to struggle. Now I could buy a few things that I had always put off before.

On the other hand, I was being watched. If my spending habits changed appreciably, I'd be nailed. The mobsters wouldn't bother about the fine points of whether I had a legitimate inheritance. No. They'd see the extra scratch and assume the worst.

Then again, I had no cash on hand. In fact, I was more leveraged than usual. My credit card and bank accounts were overdrawn and I had to wait until Monday for my paycheck (which was already spent). It looked like hardware store time again.

But I didn't want to work at the hardware store. I had done it for too long. The money accumulated *so slowly*. It went out quickly and came in slowly.

I looked at my wrist. I was wearing my new watch (though I had considered hiding it in my sock drawer to avoid suspicion). It was time for afternoon cross-country practice. This weekend we'd have a big invitational meet in Poolesville. My boys were ready. I always bring runners along slowly to peak at the end of the season. Last Friday, when we ran in Rockville, the boys did better than I'd expected. Big meets do strange things to runners.

When the pressure is on, most boys choke. Now, would I choke with this mobster thing? Could I take the surveillance? Could I stand working at the hardware store?

The race was on. In cross-country, the scoring is done by adding up the places of your five best runners. The lowest score wins. A perfect score would be $1 + 2 + 3 + 4 + 5 = 15$. I teach my boys to run in groups. That way, the team score is lower. The more talented boys pull the less talented along with them. Only at the end do they separate for that final "kick."

Today, the cold rain was taking it out of them. The disadvantage of group running is that failure, too, can be catching. My boys were not themselves in the rain. Fair-weather runners, I guess. When the going got tough . . . well, let's just say my boys didn't get anywhere. I was disgusted.

Why? I could say because of everything, but that wouldn't be descriptive enough. I could say that Scooter Martin had a lousy day, so the first group was slogging along with the second group, but that wasn't it, either. It wasn't one single thing. I was inclined to make my runners run back to the school. That's what my high school coach did to us when we ran lousy. He'd ride back in the empty bus while we jogged home. Poor meet, sore feet. Ten miles or more. It didn't matter to him. Today, they'd probably have my job for a stunt like that. So I let my team ride home with me on the bus. The only boy I wasn't mad at was Aziz, with his bad leg. He didn't have to come – especially in the rain. But he had. Son of a diplomat or something. He stood solitary in the rain without an umbrella cheering his teammates on.

A run home in the rain would have done the rest of them good. (Though, come to think of it, I don't know if it ever did me any good.) But I still needed my job. My bills wouldn't wait until February, when I'd see my first quarterly interest check on the bankers' fund (I still hadn't had confirmation on this, despite three phone calls to Bernie's secretary). Meanwhile, I was getting soaked. The bills were piling up, and I was considering selling my watch back to Nick. Couldn't Bernie let loose a few hundred? But I could never get a hold of Bernie. Suddenly he was "unavailable."

Back at the school, I didn't feel like talking to the boys, so I wrote the weekend workouts on the locker room blackboard. Then I closed up and started home in the rain. Aziz asked me if I wanted a ride. But I didn't. I wanted the cold rain to chill my bones.

When I arrived on my street, I came upon a man standing in front of my apartment door. I no longer cared. Let them take me. Lock me up with the horses forever.

"Mr O'Meara?" he said.

"Yes."

"I represent your ex-wife, Sara."

It was then that I noticed his blue blazer and charcoal gray pants: the uniform of the semisuccessful in Washington. He was short and muscular. His hair was Marine-cut short and spiked. I got out my key and tried to get around the s.o.b. He wasn't moving. "We understand that your financial picture has suddenly changed. This is something we have to talk about."

"I'm not in a talking mood." I tried to sidle past him again, but blue-gray wasn't moving. He was more solid than he looked. I had no hope against this storm trooper, "You have five minutes," I said. "Then I'm calling the police."

Seated in my living room, the man made his case. Sara, it seemed, was entitled to revisit her settlement if the circumstances that existed while we were married altered in any way. "Now, your relatives were living while you and Sara were married . . ."

"Mr . . . I never caught your name."

"M. William Tweed. Here's my card."

I took the card. "Mr Tweed. Rhymes with greed." I smiled. "I'm still in the process of making arrangements to invest this money. But I don't see why I should cut Buddy Braegen in on this. I mean they live in a house in Potomac and I'm in this cramped apartment. She should be giving *me* money!"

"Those are side issues, Mr O'Meara. The law is the law. Now, if you want to settle amicably, we could avoid costly litigation."

He handed me a document.

Oh could we? *We* means *ye*. There are a lot of other things *we* could do. *We* could take your document and *we* could shove it. But *we* might find that rather uncomfortable. "What do you expect me to do with this?"

"Sign it," said Greed.

"Before I read it?"

"You can read it any time. But I really need a signature, if that's convenient." Now it was Greed's turn to smile. I wondered if he knew Bernie.

"I'll take this under advisement, Mr Greed."

"That's Tweed. Tweed with a *T*."

I rose and began ushering him out the door. "I've got to show this to my counsel for approval first. You understand, don't you, Mr Greed – I mean Mr T."

Before he could reply, he was out the door. This time he was easy to move. I dead-bolted the lock immediately, so he could hear its definitive *thunk*. Then I went to the back fire escape. I had to walk.

A Story of Sara

Sara always liked the fast crowd. When she was a teenager, it was the rock-and-roll drug scene and Lance Romance, or, rather, Lance Erickson, lead guitarist with a group, The Dead-Ends, which was prominent regionally. They were "going places." If you listened to the band's agent, Billy Bardo, they were just one step away from a spot on *American Bandstand*.

Sara had just finished high school – even though she'd skipped about half her classes in the final semester. (It was hard to flunk out at Blair.) At eighteen, Sara was Lance's "old lady" and on the road with him and his band. She wasn't missed by her divorced mother, who was deep in therapy and couldn't see her way out of it. After another year of the shrink, she checked out, permanently. None of this sank in with Sara immediately. She was going places with Lance.

Unfortunately, the places she was going were always the same. The Dead-Ends were a warm-up act for larger bands. But then the rhythm guitar man (the most talented musician in the group) hopped over to one of the groups they opened for. His replacement was a deadhead in the end game of a heroin habit.

The band missed a couple gigs, and then they entered another world. No longer could they imagine themselves on the same stage as Bruce Springstein or U2. For them, it was grimy bars smelling of whores. Things were getting impossible. Then Lars was born, and Sara made up some story about "family money" to lure Lance away from the band and back to Silver Spring. Lance hung out there for three years, teaching guitar to rich young women Sara found for him. She scheduled the lessons and kept the books. But he didn't *only* practice guitar with them. He had another harmony in mind: "Slam bam. And don't forget to grease the hand."

Sara was powerless. She didn't like being Lance's pimp, but she didn't have much of a choice. It was either that or get a job.

Then she read about a college that gave credit for "life experiences." She went for it and lasted only one term. Though she had plenty of life experiences, those experiences didn't quite enable her to keep up with the pace of academia. Still, she admired learning and decided that she should list the school as her alma mater. After all, what's a few credits among friends?

Then it was back to the social scene: being number three (after Lance and his "students"). Keeping Lance supplied with paying pupils. Paying the bills. Surviving in reality. Telling others just the opposite. It was at this time that she entered another stratum of Washington's social life. She decided that she must find a source of networking so that she might succeed in the Washington game of cronyism. With a determined spirit and easy virtue she might *be somebody*! She was starting to make some breakthroughs of her own when Lance took off with one of his pupils. Her networking culture required a husband. This put her back to the beginning.

The rain was letting up by the time I got to church. Father McGinnis took confessions on Saturday afternoons. But with the rain, business was slow.

"Michael, what brings you by? Surely not weekly confession."

"I'd like to chat. Have a minute?"

Father Mac looked around the empty church. Then back at me. "I think I have a minute. Let's go over to the rectory, where I can have a smoke." Confession hour would be over ten minutes early that day.

Father Mac was a big man: tall and burly. He was hardly ever seen out of his clerical black. On those rare occasions he wore civilian clothes, they were usually a red plaid shirt and tan trousers.

We sat down in leather chairs that were minus some stuffing. Father Mac unfastened his collar, reached for a cigarette, and lit it. With the cigarettes and the booze, I always had a feeling that Father Mac was not long for this world. After a couple of drags, he turned his cherubic face in my direction and said, "What is it now? Thoughts of your father again?"

"No. I mean yes. You see, it's very complicated."

"It always is. Let me tell you a story about when I was at General Seminary in New York. I liked a good joke, you know. Still do. But, then, I was just a student. Well, there was this little comedy club just next to Pace University, on the edge of Chinatown. I used to perform at their 'star search' contests. I figured that if I didn't make it as a priest, I needed to have a backup.

"Well, one evening I went on after this black guy in drag. He was very funny. I knew I didn't have a chance. I started my routine, which was built around my parents and our unorthodox home life. Well, that night, my timing was off or something. My jokes just weren't funny. In fact, they struck me as sad. Poignant, you know. And suddenly I was breaking up. Not laughing, but crying. Right up there on the stage. About that time, I realized it wasn't working so I cut to the end and sat down. Then I thought, strange, there hadn't been any catcalls. I looked around and saw that my audience was tuned in, that everyone was crying. The management called a break and gave me a check and asked me to leave – *permanently*." The cigarette was finished.

While Father Mac poured three fingers of Bushmills into a tall glass and added seltzer, I tried to understand the point of the story.

"You know, they wouldn't have cried if that guy ahead of me hadn't been so funny," he said, taking a sip of his drink.

"Father, do you like wristwatches?"

"Do I like wristwatches? What kind of question is that? Of course I like wristwatches because without them I'd be late for Mass."

"That's not what I meant. I'm talking about fine jewelry."

"Well, fine jewelry can be good or it can be bad." Father Mac poured another two fingers. "Quality things in life that give us pleasure shouldn't be rejected out of hand. The Lord gave us whiskey and fine watches and other trinkets to satisfy our longing for perfection which is only understood in the abstract through God." Father Mac put down his glass and took out his hanky and blew his nose. He looked down at the floor as if there were something else on his mind. Then he smiled reflexively and turned back to me. "Michael, me boy, you ask a lot of hard questions. I don't have all the answers I should have, but let me tell you this: it's not the trinkets themselves that are troublesome, but our attitudes about them." He paused and poured himself another drink. Then he surveyed the invisible landscape and looked back up to me, "Does that make any sense?"

I said it did, but it didn't. I know that we hear stories from everyone. It's the way most of us communicate deep thoughts. I didn't know what I expected from Father McGinnis but I left him before he'd finished his drink, and before I had a chance to unburden myself. He had a way of dealing with people: taking their baggage while he walked with them. His job consumed him. Not this time. I brought to my mind Father Mac in front of a nightclub making his pitch and having it all fall flat.

When I left the rectory, I saw that the rain had stopped. I walked to the Tastee Diner for a bite to eat. Meat loaf and chicken potpie were the blue-plate specials. I had liver and onions. Father Mac always loved the liver at the Tastee Diner. Called it "holy liver," since they "cooked the *hell* out of it." What you can't eat, you can use to patch your shoes. I wondered why I hadn't invited him to join me.

I decided to make a list of things to do:

1   Go through the box of Dad's things.
2   Do class prep for the week.
3   Schedule workouts for the week.
4   Write Bernie about getting copies of the papers.
5

I couldn't think of a number five.

I skipped Mass and read the *New York Times*. In the afternoon, I went over to the school and swam a mile in the pool.

12 St Georges Ave
London, N 7
November 6, 1990

Dear Michael,

Please write. It's been lonely here. I've been doing a lot of library work and compiling lots of notes. Next week I meet with Dr Mauberley.

It's interesting to work all day – just you and the books (plus an occasional bookworm). But the silence surrounds you. It exaggerates all your feelings – like a parabolic mirror distorts your body. It can be difficult to find a balance under such circumstances.

Have you read the Valediction poems of Donne? There are four: "A Valediction: forbidding mourning," "A Valediction: of weeping," "A Valediction: of my name in the window," and "A Valediction: of the book." I believe these will somehow figure in the thesis I'll develop.

I miss you. I hope the year goes quickly.

Love,
Aisling

"I miss you." The words comforted me as I went to sleep.

Thursday. November 15. Morning workouts were over, and our next meet was the county championship. Life was coming at me, and so was Angie.

"You know I'm related to the Lees of Virginia."

Who wasn't? I shook my head.

"Of course, it was on my mother's side. Which explains the Italian surname."

I wondered what the genealogy lesson was for. We were seated together on my sofa with only a file folder between us. I could have killed Mookie. You see, I was supposed to meet with Angie after school to finish the planning of this Renaissance special event I'd promised I'd help her with. We'd intended to discuss it downtown, at the education center at GW (George Washington University) – I didn't know GW that well, but Angie had gotten her masters there (*while* working full time, she told me again and again) – but Angie's car was in the shop and mine . . . well, when we walked out into the high school parking lot, we discovered that mine had been taken.

Mookie.

"Shall we call the police?" Angie said.

"No. It's just a friend of mine who's a little free with 'borrowing.'" The police were the last people I wanted in on this. Who knew if those racetrack thugs were watching me at this very moment?

Those are the words I had used earlier that day to Bernie's receptionist. I got Angie to proctor a test for me (she was only too happy to do so), which took place right before my free period, and then I slipped out of school and went over to Bernie's office.

Like "open sesame," the words worked like magic, and lo and behold Bernie appeared and led Ali Baba into his cave, where he and the other forty thieves spirited away people's money.

"It's a crazy story, I know," I said, seated in front of his large desk, "but I went to the track and made a few bets, and now I'm being followed." I laughed, but Bernie wasn't laughing.

"What possessed you to go to the track? That doesn't sound like a high school history teacher." Bernie leaned back in his leather desk chair.

And what is a high school history teacher *supposed* to do? I was seeing a new side to Bernie. He suddenly seemed vulnerable. But I didn't want the man investing my money to be vulnerable.

"A friend of a friend took me. We were at a party." I didn't feel like telling Bernie all the details. "And, you know, we got the proverbial 'hot tip.'"

"*Hot tip?* You've got to watch hot tips, old salt." Bernie adjusted his suspenders. I suppose he thought that if they lay on his torso at a certain angle he'd look twenty pounds lighter. When they were just right, he leaned forward across his desk smiling, almost laughing – a mood transformation brought on by his suspender manipulation, perhaps – and said, "And who was it that gave you this hot tip?"

I looked him square in the eye but he looked away. "Why do you want to know?"

"Hey, is there anything to hide?" He laughed again, hoisted himself up from his chair, and walked over to his floor-length window so that he became a silhouette against the afternoon November sun. "Maybe I want to go to the track, too."

"Not with my money," I said too quickly. It was a mistake, and I knew it. I quickly added, "Look Bernie, I'd tell you if I knew. A friend of a friend. That's all I remember. But I don't like being questioned, and I don't like the feeling that people are monitoring my spending habits."

"That's their way, you know. An old trick, really. Watch for changes in lifestyle. Most people who get money want to spend it, can't abide the thought of their money just sitting there when it could be out there bringing its owner little goodies." The silhouette was rubbing his hands together. Then he emerged from the light. "Of course, old salt, that makes *my* money management program for you even better."

"You mean not doing anything with my principal?"

"Correction. Not *spending* your principal. Delayed gratification. The only way to get anywhere in life, Mike."

"But do you think I should go to the police?"

"No. No. I don't think there's anything to gain by bringing them into the picture. Nothing to gain at all. Look, you came to Dr Bernie for a prescription, and my advice is this: stay away from the track and don't change your lifestyle. Everything will be fine in the morning."

Bernie was now hustling me out the door. He figured I'd made clear my reason for being in his office, and he'd decided that it was innocuous.

"About my investments, Bernie . . ."

"Not to worry. They've already been made and recorded."

"Can I have a copy of those records?"

"Certainly, I'll have my secretary do it for you and mail it out."

We were at the gatekeeper's station. She was usually an iron-willed lady, but just then she seemed nervous. "You've got an appointment, Mr Krupt. It's Mr Delgato." She tried to say "Delgato" quietly, but that only drew my attention to the name. Bernie changed his mood again. He was all dispatch now.

"Bernie, my copies?"

"Oh, Miss Fee will take care of that."

And then he was gone. I didn't see anyone else in the waiting room. Probably a private entrance. I dropped my eyes to the iron lady.

"Do you want something?"

"Mr Krupt said you'd make me copies of my investment file."

She made a noise with her tongue and bent over her work again.

"Excuse me, Miss Fee."

Without looking up, she inhaled sharply. "I'm busy right now."

"And I have to get back to work."

This time she looked me in the eye, but threateningly. "If you want your copies you'll have to make them yourself. I certainly don't have the time." She pushed herself up and disappeared into a back room, presumably to retrieve my file.

That suited me fine. That way there'd be no screening.

Five minutes later, file in hand, I was directed to the photocopier, located in a small room lit by fluorescents. As I made copies of each document in the folder, I noticed a common logo on most of the cover pages: a horse jumping over the Capitol Building and the initials C.V. at the bottom. I didn't think too much of it though. I was running close for my sixth-period American History class and I had to get back to the school.

Then I heard footsteps from behind Bernie's door. I froze. I was almost finished. I wanted to copy it all so that I could see what was happening. But I know Bernie had expected me to wait until Miss Fee found the time to do the copying – probably never. He'd be furious if he knew what I was doing now. These copiers are so slow. I dropped a page on the floor and almost knocked over the folder. I thought I heard Miss Fee stirring. I had to finish quickly. I had to get out of there before Iron Fee could nail me. I know Bernie hadn't meant for me to copy *all* of it.

Then the long green light-tube beneath the plate of glass made its last trip back. In moments I'd have it. I was breathing pretty hard. Maybe they'll hear me and come racing in. Finished. I lifted up the cover and shoved the original back into the folder and left it atop the machine. I flew to the door and, when it closed, began running.

The papers were in my hand. In no special order. I'd sort them out later. Later. Later. "You've got to confront these things," Father Mac had once said. "If you don't, they'll confront *you*. They'll change you in ways you may not like." The big man had lit a cigarette then. It was the middle of summer. His shirt was stained with sweat. But he didn't seem to mind. He took the heat as it came and used air-conditioning only for sleeping.

I made it back to school and almost knocked Angie down in the hall.

"Michael, what's the rush? Look at you – you're full of per-spiration. Did you decide to run your team's cross-country course?" She laughed.

"No time now, Angie. Thanks for watching the test. I'll get to you later."

When my day was over – just before practice – I glanced at the file. It seemed that my money was in three places: a banker's fund and a money market deposit at Old Republic Savings and Loan, stock in Capital Ventures, and a commercial note to Schmidt Properties. What struck me was that the logo I'd noticed on most of the papers seemed to stand for Capital Ventures, Ltd. Did this mean that all my money was really in *one* place? I didn't have time to speculate. It was time for cross-country.

"You know we've really never had a chance to get acquainted very well," said Angie in a low voice that certainly didn't come from the Lees of Virginia. She readjusted herself on my couch. Only the file folder between us separated her from me.

Angie took off her glasses. Her face reminded me of someone. It was a full face, though Angie was generally slim.

"I was working on my master's, you see. Takes four terms or twelve courses plus a thesis. I was at it almost four years. That makes a dent in your social life, I can tell you," Angie delivered these words with aristocratic pride.

"What about Bob?" Bob Crouter was a math teacher who also ran the computer lab at the school. Though I didn't keep up on such things, I had assumed that Angie and Bob were going together.

"Oh, Bob's more interested in computers than in people. He's got a side consulting business, you know. Works all the time."

I nodded.

She strummed her fingertips on my shoulder. I felt her long nails through my clothes. What did long fingernails mean? I looked at her hand and then back up her arm to her face. Her face was lightly powdered. Sara used to powder her face, too. Aisling didn't.

"What was your thesis on?" I asked.

"History and Poetry in the English Civil War: The Poetry of John Denham."

"That's a mouthful."

"Fascinating, really. It was a period of revolution."

I looked into Angie's eyes. "You're a revolutionary, then?"

She laughed.

Then Angie kissed me. Her lips were tighter than I'd expected. A light touch of the lips, then gentle exploring. Our bodies were moving closer when the file folder that was between us fell and spilled its contents out onto the floor. We broke our embrace and laughed.

But it really wasn't funny. My humor had just been a screen to stop me from thinking. What I most wanted to forget was my father's death. I reconstructed the file.

"So how did you hear about my legacy?" I asked Angie when we had gathered the Shakespeare papers and moved into the kitchen for some coffee.

"Oh that. I was just teasing you. I'm not very good at social *intercourse* – you know, conversation."

I knew what she meant. "But how did you find out?"

"Oh, a woman came by the school for you."

"A woman? What did she look like?"

"Long curly hair. Very white skin. Short. A little heavy."

"Sounds like Sara."

"Your ex-wife?"

"How'd you know?"

"She said you'd been avoiding her because you came into a bundle and that she'd get her hands on some of it."

"That's Sara."

"Sounds like a saint."

"Oh yeah?"

"Well, you know. Money corrupts. She's just interested in saving your soul."

I poured the coffee.

So we planned: Shakespeare and history. Together. We spread out our papers on the Formica kitchen table and got to work.

"What I think would be interesting is to get the students first to discover the great obsession that Shakespeare had with the Wars of the Roses."

"Obsession?" I replied.

"Certainly. Look, he wrote the two Henry the Fourth plays, Henry the Fifth, the three Henry the Sixth plays, and then there's Richard the Third. They all fit in with the Wars of the Roses. That's seven plays. Shakespeare only wrote ten history plays. That's 70 percent! And he only wrote thirty-seven or thirty-eight plays all together (depending on what you think of *The Two Noble Kinsmen*). That's about 20 percent of his corpus. I'd call that an obsession."

I shrugged my shoulders. I guess I would, too. Then I told her about what I'd found about the historical Sir John Oldcastle, Lord Cobham, who was a notorious character and was later executed for heresy in 1417. Later his reputation improved and he was regarded as a martyr. I offered to set up a teaching unit on this story and how Shakespeare decided to change from Oldcastle to

Falstaff – perhaps because he feared Sir William Brooke, seventh Baron Cobham.

Angie liked the idea and quickly thumbed in her dog-eared volume of Shakespeare to some handwritten notes she'd made from the Prologue to *The Life of Sir John Hardcastle*, an Elizabethan play once mistakenly attributed to Shakespeare:

> Nor aged counselor to youthful sin,
> But one whose virtue shone above the rest,
> A valiant martyr and a virtuous peer.

It was agreed that I would create four such units in the sequence covering key segments in the fifteenth century and drawing political parallels when I could to the US in the twentieth century. The point was to find out why the Wars of the Roses were so historically significant that Shakespeare was driven to write about them in so much detail.

Angie was not what I'd expected. As usual, I had been a poor judge of character.

When we were through, Angie gathered her things.

"I enjoyed this," I said lightly touching her cheek with my open hand.

"It will be good for the kids."

"Screw the kids."

Angie smiled and guided my hand from her face. "You have a beautiful watch, Michael. I think I've seen those in jewelry ads."

I smiled. I really missed my father.

Chapter Five

Val-e-dic-tion / ˌva-lə-ˈdikshən/. A bidding farewell; a leave taking: Latin, from *vale* (farewell) + *dicere* (to say).

Let me powre forth
My teares before thy face, whil'st I stay here
For thy face coines them, and thy stampe they beare,
And by this Mintage they are something worth,
  For thus they bee
  Pregnant of thee;
Fruits of mych griefe they are, emblemes of more,
When a teare falls, that thou falst which it bore,
So thou and I are nothing then, when on a divers shore.

  On a round ball
A workeman that hath copies by, can lay
An Europe, Afrique, and an Asia,
And quickly make that, which was nothing, *All*,
  So doth each teare,
  Which thee doth weare,
A globe, yea world by that impression grow,
Till thy teares mixt with mine doe overflow
This world, by waters sent from thee, my heaven dissolved so.

  O more then Moone,
Draw not up seas to drowne me in thy spheare,

Weepe me not dead, in thine armes, but forbeare
To teach the sea, what it may doe too soone.
        Let not the winde
        Example finde,
To doe me more harme then it purposeth;
Since thou and I sigh one anothers breath,
Who e'r sighes most, is cruellest, and hasts the others death.

I went back to the used bookstore and bought John Donne's *Songs and Sonnets*. I've said before, I prefer facts to poetry. But I did like the details of this poem. Ash had recommended it to me. The reflection of a face in a tear. A miniature. A reflection. A copy. Yet more real than the copies of globes that are meant to show us the world as it is.

My father had a globe he kept in the living room. It sat on a stand and could be tilted and rotated. The countries on that globe are mostly changed by now: French North Africa, the Belgian Congo, the entire subcontinent of India, Tibet, and Siam. What kind of globe was this? A reflection of a moment in history.

When friends are separated, is it like the obsolete globe? How small the tear. How great the world. But do we not, from our viewpoint, judge our own vicissitudes as cosmically important? Is this hubris or merely fact?

A Story of Aisling – Part One

The first time I saw Aisling was at a Humanities meeting at the high school. They were introducing new teachers, and when they mentioned her name and she stood up, I was struck by three things.

The first was her appearance and demeanor. She was of medium height, but looked much taller. Her skin was clear and very white – almost porcelain in appearance. Her hair was strawberry blond and sort of frizzy. She rose from her chair in such a way that her stature seemed to increase and increase. Immediately, I knew that she was not the sort of person who should teach at Lazy Fair. "I'll give her one year," I thought. This one certainly will not make it here. Too smart. Too much of an attitude. And she has principles.

A person like that doesn't last here.

Montgomery County, Maryland, is a huge school district comprising more than a dozen high schools. When you consider that each high school has two or three feeder middle schools, and that each middle school has two or three feeder elementary schools, then you can get a sense of how big the county school district is. A district that big requires standardization. This rule flows from the public's thirst for "accountability." *We want to know if those damn teachers are doing their jobs! Are they teaching our children everything they should know?* The concept of "everything they should know" has expanded in affluent areas such as Montgomery County. It now includes not only proficiency in the academic subjects such as history, English, math, and science, but also in being a good citizen and a good person, and establishing habits necessary to lead an honorable, virtuous life. All this teachers must accomplish on a starting salary that is only three thousand dollars a year above the income a family of four must not exceed in order to qualify to receive food stamps.

When the rich parents began checking out of their kids' lives in order to maximize their own personal development/enjoyment/pleasure, then the burden was shifted to the schools. A parent's responsibility is merely to have the child, to be able to pay for the roof over that child's head, to dress the child in designer clothes, and to deposit him or her on school property at a given time. The rest is given over to the schools (or the live-in nannies for those who can afford them).

This was an impossible and unreasonable assignment. Thus the proper candidate for a teaching position at Lazy Fair high school had to be able to block all of this out and turn a deaf ear to those parents who put forth their unreasonable expectations as the standard of good teaching. By her body language, Aisling struck me as unwilling to be some parent's punching bag. She didn't even look to be the sort of person who would fake it.

Second, the Montgomery County school district presented teachers a curriculum that had to be followed to the letter. When I was a teacher at King High School, the department made up its own curriculum according to the needs of its particular students. We revised it every three years so that we kept "in touch." The parents of those kids were grateful for a creative teacher who might inspire his or her child out of the poverty they lived in. Not so at Lazy Fair. Fairview parents wanted copies of the school district's central office curriculum on how to teach history. These parents referred to these edicts (created by bureaucrats who were failures as teachers and so were promoted to administration) whenever their child got a low grade, and used them to build a case against the teacher.

Only a career bureaucrat would assent to such authoritarianism. It drained every ounce of creativity from you. However, I had agreed to the contract. I had submitted myself to the yoke. But Aisling? This new teacher with the frizzy, strawberry blond hair? She would have to fight or flee. She was not made for this. Too much her own person. She'd never put up with it.

Finally, what struck me was her reserve. She did not sit next to anyone at the meeting but, instead, off by herself. This was a person who would never fit into the mediocre clique that made up the Fairview faculty.

Well, I'd seen teachers come and go at Lazy Fair. In fact, I'd created criteria that enabled me to guess whether history would repeat itself. This was what historians did. I pretended to be an historian. QED.

Aisling would be gone in a year. I felt sure of this.

After making my judgment about her future, I paused and looked to where she had been sitting. She was gone. And I asked myself whether she had really been there or not. Had she merely been a porcelain figment of my imagination?

It was November 22nd, Thanksgiving. One year ago I had spent the day with Aisling. Two years ago, I volunteered at a soup kitchen. Sara and I had just broken up. This year, I was sitting in the living room of Vic Santini, listening to stories of his years in the construction business. Angie and her mother were working in the kitchen.

Vic was a paunchy old blowhard, but some of his stories were interesting. The man knew development, and how power tilted in that area. I asked him if he'd ever heard of Schmidt Properties.

He screwed up his face. "Where did you hear about that one?"

"Oh, I got a tip that it was a good private investment."

"Pha! Well, whoever told you that is a lying son-of-a-bitch. That's a mob operation, and in this market it could fall apart at any moment."

I swallowed hard. "Are you sure?"

"You haven't given them any money yet, have you?"

"Oh no," I replied trying to keep my voice level.

"Well, don't. Commercial real estate. Projects that should never have been built. And substandard materials to boot!"

I sat there trying to take it all in. Old Vic was looking me over. "You've given them money, haven't you?"

I grimaced and shrugged.

"What was it, a limited partnership?"

"No. Actually, I went to school with a guy who became an investment adviser."

"Not a lawyer, I hope."

Again I grimaced. "I guess I don't know much about this sort of thing, Mr Santini."

The old man pulled his chair close to mine and put his hand on my shoulder. "Look, Michael, there is no reason why you *should* know these things. What happened? Get an inheritance?"

I nodded.

"That's the way it always is. You work hard in a decent job, like my little Angie. Teacher. Good people, teachers. But the way of the world is that good people get taken by bad people. It's the way of life. Your lawyer buddy probably owns some of Schmidt Properties himself. He used your money to buy back all or some of his own investment. You gave him instant liquidity."

"But that's stealing."

"Damn right. But he'd never do time for it because you got something for your money. You got some percentage of something."

"But what I have is worthless."

"It doesn't matter if your something is nothing – just as long as it is something."

What could I say?

"Your money's down the toilet."

I tried to smile with no effect.

"Look, you don't last forty years in the construction business without knowing how to deal with funny money and the bozos with their bazookas. Cheer up. I think the turkey is just about ready."

"The body of Christ; the bread of Heaven."

I took the wafer and chewed it carefully. What was this all about? What was happening to my life? I had Sara thirsting for money. Bernie had my money. Angie wanted something. Ash was off in London. Mookie was "borrowing" my car somehow. And where was Michael O'Meara in all this? My wholeness was fractured. I had to find some way to put it back together.

It was nice to imagine I'd be "set" for life. But would I really be set? Would I become like the wife in the fairy tale "The Fisherman and his Wife," whose successive wishes became larger and more grandiose until she wants to be God? Where does desire meet pride and become sin? I really didn't understand, but clearly my studies in history were replete with examples of generals and politicians whose desires escalated to a point that they destroyed them. (As in the inscription on the solitary ruin in the Shelley poem went: "My name is Ozymandias, King of Kings, / Look on my works, ye Mighty, and despair!" Alone and insignificant among the shifting sands, the monument belied its message.)

Speaking of contradictory messages, you may wonder why I claim to be indifferent to poetry and yet I read it, memorize it, and even cite it from time to time. It is one more item on my list of inexplicables. I guess poetry is an expression of last resort. You don't use it unless you're driven to it. But even poetry could not express the feelings I had earlier at the county cross-country championships.

It was one of those November days that can't make up its mind. During warm-ups and the girls' race, it was generally fair: fifty degrees and calm. Then, in the interval between races, a wind arose and dropped the temperature. By the middle of the boys' four-mile race, it had to be in the low forties, with a wind chill in the twenties.

My thinclads (that's what they call cross-country runners) were running bravely, but it was a difficult day to run. Aziz's leg injury forced him to quit after two miles. My first group of Scooter and Billy Joe were doing fine, but my second group had started faster than they should have. Now, with the wind and cold, they were tying up fast. I watched them decelerate over the last mile.

Then Sam Washington, the only African American on the team, made a gutsy move. Sam varied between number five and number six on the team, but now he was running just ahead of Lo Choi, our third runner. Sam was literally pulling our second group after him. All the rest had given up, but not Sam.

It was inspiring to watch him over that last quarter mile. He turned it on. He was blasting through a Nordic head wind, but he was moving faster and faster. He passed seventeen runners. I could see a crowded finish so I rushed to the chute.

Now, the end of a cross-country race requires that officials mark out the exact order of finish. This is necessary for team scoring. With ten schools each sending seven runners, this could become a problem. Therefore, at the end of a race a funnel is set up, marked off by ropes.

As many as four boys could fit at the head of the funnel (or "chute"). The chute then quickly tapered to a width that could accommodate only one. The race ends at the finish line, but the scoring occurs at the end of the chute. In competitive races, many runners try to improve their position in the chute. An aggressive boy who finished twentieth might nonetheless end up with card seventeen (indicating that he'd finished seventeenth).

I saw Sam's eyes when he was ten yards away from the finish line. The lad was almost unconscious. He ran into the chute and stumbled. Other boys were pushing past him. So I jumped into the chute and pushed right back. What an uproar this caused! Other coaches jumped in, too. It was chaos.

In the end, at least three people whom Sam had beaten were judged to have been ahead of him. This made the difference in the race. Our school came in second.

I was proud of my boys, and especially of Sam. The quiet kid with the least natural talent of any of my runners had made the meet memorable for me. I tried to tell him what I thought, but I didn't express myself well.

When I got up at the end of Mass on Sunday, I was full of resolve. I had prayed for my father. I had decided that my priorities were upset. I wanted to affect others, the way Sam Washington had affected me.

I lingered toward the back of the line of parishioners filing out.

"Are you free this afternoon, Father?"

"I'm going to Loaves and Fishes, I'm afraid, Michael."

Loaves and Fishes was a soup kitchen staffed by volunteers. I didn't feel like going so I smiled, shook his hand, and left.

It was time for a walk.

I went down Wisconsin, to the Galleria again. I don't know if it was a conscious decision but something about the place drew me. Would that snooty watch salesman be there? If I went back, would he recognize my new watch as a fake – or be impressed, as Angie was?

As I walked among the glittering items in the mall, I sought to understand their allure. I ventured outside and had a croissant and a coffee at a small sidewalk café. While sitting there, I noticed a real estate office across the street. It looked open. I didn't finish my coffee.

In the window were photographs of beautiful homes. Expensive homes.

"Can I help you?" a man in a navy sports coat and charcoal pants asked me. He was standing outside the agency smoking a cigarette.

"Just looking," I replied.

"What price range are you looking at?"

"I'm not too concerned about price," I replied. Instantly, the man wilted and started to turn away in disgust. I suppose that's the real tip-off that you're only a window shopper. Anyone with serious money on the table has a price range (even if it's in the stratosphere). This was turning out to be just like the watch salesman. I wasn't going to let that happen twice. "I've just gotten a large inheritance, you see. Therefore, money is no object."

Instantly, the salesman sprang back to life.

"Would you like to go on a tour?"

How could I refuse?

My guide told me that Schmidt Properties was strictly a commercial firm. He didn't know much about it. His attention was on the "estates" he was about to show me. These homes were to be had for a "steal" in today's "buyer's market." I looked at the homes he took me to. They seemed swollen. Typically, they sat on a cleared tract of land no bigger than a city lot. They were surrounded by other, similarly swollen houses. Most were three stories with three-car garages and five to seven thousand feet of living space. Unfortunately, after a house like this was constructed, there was not much lot left. Fence in the three-foot border around your monster. Who cares! You've got a dream. Semicircular "coach driveways" fronted each of these pretentious palaces.

My guide didn't blink when he told me the prices. "Seven-fifty or eight hundred thousand."

I know it's 1990, but really, these prices seemed preposterous. "A lot of money for no lot."

"They *were* selling for double that before the . . . ah . . . market adjustment."

"They were selling, but they didn't sell, did they? That means they were overpriced."

The salesman did not respond.

I must admit that sunken baths in multichambered bedroom suites (that were larger than my apartment) made me pause. I liked them. I wanted them. I knew that I could *get used to* the pampered life that big money provided. No more calculations on how I would stretch a dinner for three nights. No more "roach motels" to rid my home of unwanted pests: in these big houses there were no pests. Pests weren't even allowed in the servants' entrance.

When my guide dropped me off back at the Galleria, my head spun with trade names: types of marble, security systems, and retractable skylights.

I was now in the mood for Christmas shopping.

12 St Georges Ave

London, N 7

November 29, 1990

Dear Michael,

Which do I prefer? John Donne, the rake, or Father Donne, the Dean of St Paul's? What a case of split personalities. In some way,

---

the Valediction poems offer a link between these two. They are written by Donne, the younger, with the spirit and mind of Donne, the elder.

As I develop my analysis of these I will keep you informed.

My director, Dr Hugh Selwyn Mauberley, is the most intelligent man I've ever met. I began reading some of his own writing so that I could understand him more as a person. The man is fascinating. One of his central tenets is that art is decaying because of the presence of money. The pure power of art's ability to express becomes perverted when the marketplace makes decisions that should be left to those who *know*. Hugh is really very elegant in his exposition. You should hear him sometime. He's a man who leaves an impression.

Aisling

When I read this letter, a few things struck me: One, her tone seemed more formal. Two, she called her director fascinating, and three, I wondered what kind of *impression* Dr Mauberley was making on her. For that matter, I wondered what kind of *impression* Angie was making on me! I noticed that she forgot to write 'love.'

"Coach?" It was Sam Washington, come to see me during my free period.

"Have a seat, Sam."

The boy straddled the chair so that his chin rested on the chair back.

"I wanted to thank you."

"For what?"

"In the meet. Sticking up for me. Those officials were out to get me."

"They weren't very good."

"Oh, *I* think they knew what they were doing."

I couldn't comment further. To do so would be unprofessional. A teacher is not supposed to criticize his colleagues from other schools in front of a student. Still, I couldn't help my body language.

There weren't too many African Americans in cross-country in our district. Some of the white coaches were not "in touch." Some were blatant racists. When I was younger, I used to put their bigotry in their faces. But there were more of them than there was of me. I backed off. But I never forgot.

"You ran well, Sam. It was a finish you can be proud of. If I'd been better or quicker, maybe you'd have gotten the number you deserved."

Sam looked down awhile. Then he got up to go. "Like I said. I appreciate your sticking up for me. My family – we don't forget things. *I* won't forget that. Depend upon it."

He left. I felt I didn't deserve any accolades.

"The first thing about grief is to put things in some kind of order," Father Mac said. "You've got to separate the subjective from the objective appraisal. There are natural and unnatural deaths. A natural death is when a son outlives his father. The reverse is unnatural."

"And the age of death."

"Yes. The age and means of death are all factors."

"So a person's death might be natural in some respects and unnatural in others."

"That's right. And thinking in this way gives one a perspective beyond the pain. It's that perspective that's important if you're going to incorporate the fact of a death into your life."

The fact of a death. All my family were now dead: mother, brother, and father. Dead. A fact. I guess I'd never learned to incorporate it. It had happened. And I had continued on. One tries to protect oneself from the pain. You learn strategies of avoidance. But does it ever get better? To me the question meant: could I talk about it without breaking up? The medievals believed that sighing and expressions of grief resulted in the loss of *anima*, or vital spirit. To lose some of your vital spirit hastened your own death.

I was not yet prepared to die.

I got my credit line extended for Christmas shopping. I must admit that I've never been overly keen on Christmas shopping. It seemed to be the greatest promotional gimmick of our time for retail sales. It certainly had nothing to do with the Christian feast. In fact, the season of Advent was supposed to be quiet and reflective and not overtly celebratory – as the malls and stores would have it.

No. Christmas had become a nonreligious holiday: the winter solstice festival. It coincided with a religious feast but it was separate. The confusing thing was that the religious and secular celebrations bore the same name.

Not a profound point, but it bears mentioning since this was the first year I really became consumed by my shopping. I had no family but I did *know* people. And this year I sought some kind of contact.

I made a list of people (most of whom I'd never given a gift). I took on extra hours at the hardware store. I armed myself with my plastic card and hit the malls.

This year I decided not to give practical gifts. I had once thought that a good gift was something somebody needed but wouldn't or couldn't buy for himself. This year, I was discarding that theory. Instead, I sought gifts that nobody needed. Gifts that made a statement. That were luxuries. I got clear clocks that rhythmically tilted back and forth with a viscous blue fluid moving slightly behind; Chinese balls made to massage the back; a lamp that turned on with a clap of hands; a machine that reproduced the sound of the ocean; and other exotica. My policy was to buy the gift and then match it to someone on my list. The gift came first.

It was exciting. I had never gone into some of these stores, like The Sharper Image and The Continental Yankee, because I knew they had nothing I needed. But now that *need* had been discarded, I explored everything. I felt like the mountain climber who is drawn to scale a peak "because it is there."

I wrapped all the gifts myself so I could play with them one more time before they were gone. The paper I used to wrap them was also making a statement. It was time to communicate with the world. I even bought Sara and her kids something (despite a recent letter from Tweed threatening all sorts of recriminations – short of capital punishment).

I had Christmas songs blasting while I sat in the midst of my presents, paper, and ribbon. My task was virtually complete when Mookie came by. He turned down the volume on my record player.

"Too loud for you?" I asked.

He shook his head and sat down.

"Have you been enjoying the season? Do you have any plans for Christmas? Family or anything?"

"Buddhist, remember?" he said.

"No Christmas? No gifts?"

"Look man, I've got something to tell you."

I didn't like the look on his face. He was too grim. This wouldn't do. I'd cheer him up with a special gift: a radio you could listen to underwater.

"Wait a minute, Mookie. You may not be in the mood for Christmas, but I am. Here's a gift I got *especially for you*."

I handed him the package with its silver paper and curled red ribbon.

"No man. I told you – "

"I insist!" I walked over and opened it for him. "It's an underwater radio!" I said.

He smiled. "Thanks. I didn't ask for any gift. You know we've never – "

"Don't mention it. Next time you're underwater, you can catch your favorite tunes."

Mookie turned the radio over as if he were inspecting it for flaws. Then he walked toward the door.

"Don't you want some cookies? I baked them myself."

"No man. I've got to go."

He started out the door and then came back. "I've got to tell you something."

"What?"

He shut the door and looked me right in the eye. "It's about your car, man. I wrecked it. It's totaled. Gone forever."

Chapter Six

Epiphany. The beginning of the New Year.

I received a special gift. It was from Angie's father.

I didn't spend Christmas with the Santinis. No. Christmas I spent by myself. I went to midnight Mass, came home, slept, woke up, went to a matinee movie, and then nursed a pint of Johnny Walker I'd bought for the occasion. I sat there drinking right out of the bottle and staring at the three Christmas cards/thank-you notes I'd received this year. Three for fifty. With an average like that, I'd be fired from any professional baseball team. Even the Texas League. Oh, where are those violins when you need them?

But I went with Angie to the Santini's Epiphany party. Epiphany. The feast of the Magi. Twelfth Night. Angie read from the play. She'd even baked an Epiphany cake. Angie's mom read from the Bible. Meanwhile Vic Santini read to me out of the book of life: experience.

"I've given some thought to your problem, Michael. Basically, there are only a couple of ways to fight back against a developer that I know of: the small way and the big way. *The small way* requires – how should I say – "reapportioning" building supplies at the sites, you know. What you can get your hands on. Unfortunately, this isn't as easy as it used to be, and besides, it doesn't get you much moolah.

"The second way, *the big way*, requires you to investigate very closely and find a variety of code violations that could stop or slow down key projects. You take this information to them and try to sell it for the amount they've cheated you."

My heart was uneasy with both of these alternatives. I wasn't much for stealing. Besides, action of any kind required an inner fire, which I'd always lacked. Reactive and not proactive was my style. Going above or below the law was really a side issue.

Vic noted my response. Or perhaps he anticipated it. The man leaned back in his green corduroy La-Z-Boy and folded his hands over his considerable paunch, "Of course you may not have the stomach for door number two." He paused slightly to allow me to interrupt. I waited for door number three. "Which is why I kept looking and found that Old Republic Savings and Loan is a sister company to Schmidt Properties."

How did Vic know I had money in Old Republic? I hadn't said a word to him about it. I was feeling mismatched. "But what has that got to do with anything –" I began.

"Don't you see, Michael? There's the secured/unsecured personal loan."

"What's that?"

"Look, you figure you've been screwed, blued, and tattooed, right?"

"Well, yes."

"*Well*, nothing. You accept that *first* or you're nowhere."

"Okay. Go on."

"Who did it to you?"

"This guy I know, Bernie. I told you before."

"Right. And he's in with this outfit or he wouldn't have had any of their securities. Am I right?"

I smiled and shrugged.

"And I'll bet he's in at Capital Ventures, too."

Capital Ventures. The logo on all the papers. Again, how did Vic know about that one?

"Then they're all tied together," I replied.

Vic gave me a disapproving glance. In it I read his mind: I should have known this *before* investing. I was a complete idiot who had trusted a school buddy – well, Bernie wasn't exactly a *buddy*. But at Pembroke, cheating simply hadn't been done. Why cheat? Where would that get you? Pembroke had been about fierce competition. Clean, honest. May the best man win . . .

At least that was what I had believed. But the truth was, Bernie was a manipulator – then and now. How else would he have been able to appear to be a hip revolutionary without actually being one? Now he was pretending to be an investment adviser without actually being one.

But I had called him. He hadn't made the call. I had only myself to blame. I had thought that someone I knew wouldn't cheat me. I wasn't looking for a "deal" by going to an acquaintance. I was only looking for honest advice.

But what did I know? How could I have been expected to know anything? When had I ever had money to invest? All my salary went toward paying my bills, and even then I was forever short!

My mistake had been in expecting Bernie to act as I would have acted. Yet, that was a lie, too. I *had* to be tough or be beaten by those who were.

"Old Republic and Schmidt Properties are both subsidiaries of Capital Ventures," Vic said. That means that your enemy is Capital Ventures." Vic was in his element. If I were to court his daughter – was I really courting his daughter? what about Aisling? – then I had to get balls and do what had to be done.

"When you accept that, then any subsidiary of Capital Ventures is an equal enemy." He looked to me for confirmation. I grimaced. "Listen. You can use your portfolio of securities and apply for a secured loan. After you've gotten your loan, you default."

"I don't understand." The only loans I'd ever gotten were car loans, loans from the credit card company, and guaranteed student loans (which I'd almost finished repaying).

"Look: One, go to Old Republic and take out a loan on your portfolio. What is it, by the way?"

Should I tell him? One doesn't like to talk about money, but what else were we discussing? "All the securities amount to around four hundred thousand."

"Holy shit, boy." Vic crossed himself. "If you don't do something, you'll roast in the fires of hell."

I wanted to give some thought to this, but time did not allow.

"Look, Michael. You can get a loan for eighty percent of your collateral, easy. They'll loan you three hundred and twenty thousand dollars on that, and then you never pay it back."

"But can you do that?"

"If they accept the collateral, they have to. All perfectly legal. You get the money, and they get their worthless paper back."

"But will they accept the collateral?"

"It's a sister company. They'd have to."

"But what if they don't?"

"And what if we enter into a nuclear war tomorrow? Listen, Michael, you have to stop being such a worrywart. If you want to kiss the money of your departed father good-bye – it was your father, right? – then be my guest. But I think you have a responsibility."

"My father and several others. A group accident." The words stuck in my throat. He was right. I had to fight back. "You're saying I must take out the loan and then make *them* eat it."

Vic smiled.

I almost broke a tooth on the penny in the Epiphany cake.

> This fellow is wise enough to play the fool
> And to do that well craves a kind of wit

He must observe their mood on whom he jests,
The quality of persons, and the time;
And like the haggard, check at every feather
That comes before his eye. This is a practice
As full of labor as a wise man's art;
For folly that he wisely shows is fit;
But wise men, folly-fall'n, quite taint their wit.

How would I atone for my mistakes?

Chapter Seven

Sara had been a recommendation of Lil Hamlin, a biology teacher at Fairview. "For a white woman, she's got soul," Lil had said.

How could I say no?

I was immediately attracted to Sara. She took me places I'd never been before. We went to bars that featured new and upcoming music groups. With Sara it was always important to be where the "action" was. To be with the "important" people and collect desirable acquaintances so they might be displayed for all to see. Why it was that Sara was attracted to me, I'll never know – except that I was an improvement upon her first husband, Lance Erickson (whom she called "Lance Romance"), the guitar player and father of her two children.

Compared with Lance, I was a step up in terms of education, but I was poor. At the Treasury Department, Sara earned thirty-five to my twenty-five. Together, we had sixty. But the hitch was that Sara's money was *her own* and my money was *jointly owned*. I paid the rent and utilities and anything else until my check was spent. She bought what she liked. A woman had to have clothes and go to the right places, to be seen with the Blue Book set.

At first it was exciting. I bought it all.

"Oh yes, Mike is writing an important treatise on ancient Rome. It will be very influential."

"You are? Tell us about it."

And I told them. Even though there was no monograph. That didn't matter to Sara. She was married to a budding author. This was one of the acceptable social entrees. If only I had had a tape recorder, I might have had an outline for a real book.

Then I began to find reasons to stay away from her outings and her friends. When she left me to live with Buddy, I knew our relationship had never been anything at all. Two years of my life. Two years of Sara. Two years of nothing. However, when she left, it saved my life.

I was a lifesaver once. I never liked to swim. I wasn't very good at it. But my father thought that a summer job of lifeguarding would be easy money. To be a lifeguard you have to pass a life-saving test. Now, I had taken the whole class that led up to the test. This included learning all the carries, first aid, and drown-proofing. But I was barely competent (at best). I didn't want to fail, so I decided to skip the test.

This did not pass muster with Dad.

"And why not?"

"I'm no good."

"If you were no good you'd have been kicked out of the class."

"They never kick people out of the classes."

"I should say not. They took my money easily enough. If you were horrible, they'd have been bound to tell me."

"It doesn't work that way, Dad."

"Humph. A person's got to have values."

"D-a-a-a-d."

"You're going."

"I'm not."

"You're going."

"I'll fail."

"So what?"

"I'll *fail*."

"You're going."

I went. I suppose that's the way it was sometimes. Sometimes you have to do things you don't want to.

And now I was supposed to take out a loan and *not* repay it? The whole thing didn't feel right. But doing nothing also didn't feel right.

I passed lifesaving on the first try.

A Story of Aisling – Part Two

The second time I saw Aisling was in the faculty office space that English shares with History. They call it the Humanities teachers' lounge. I rarely go into this space because I either sit in my classroom or as the cross-country coach, I retire to the locker room as my quasi office. However, for most of the faculty, this was a retreat from the importuning grade petitioners. There was a message board inside, but nine times out of ten the messages just resulted in more work.

It was in the eighth week of the term that I happened into the office/lounge for only the fourth or fifth time all term. A parent wanted to discuss an interim grade notice I had sent home. (An interim grade notice lets the parents know that, at midterm, their child is getting a D or an F in the course.) That day, I entered the office with a group of "reading notebooks," which I had to grade by Friday. I sat myself in one of the generic gray metal, white Formica–topped desks that faced the window. I liked to look out at nature, as opposed to the walls and halls that composed the school.

That was when I heard her voice. I knew it was a voice that I had heard before because I have an acute memory for auditory sensations. But whose voice it was, I wasn't sure. Then I realized it was *her* voice. And I knew that *her* voice was important to me. But that was all I knew.

I turned my head and saw her. Aisling. She was talking to her department chair, John Mears.

"I don't care if the child's father is a network news anchor and the pride of this school," she was saying. "I will not change the grade."

John Mears was a balding man approaching sixty. He'd just inherited the department chair when Margaret Caruthers and her successful stockbroker husband (fifteen years her senior) had decided that they should live in Bermuda. (Margaret had met her husband-to-be rather late in life, at around forty-eight, and had been married only seven years.) She was at the top of her retirement package, so why not?

Mears had spent years as the loyal opposition to Caruthers. He had felt that she had coddled the faculty and not "cracked the whip" to ensure discipline. I had always thought that Mears had been born out of his proper place and time. He would have loved being an operative in Fascist Italy or Nazi Germany.

"Do you know who this man is?" Mears said, as a curvy vein on his temple began to rise.

"The man is not in my class. His son is *barely* in my class." Aisling pursed her lips defiantly.

Didn't she understand that if she behaved like this Mears could make her life very difficult? This was not a politic way to proceed. My attention was riveted.

"Don't get cute with me, Aisling," Mears said.

"What did you say?"

It was a showdown, and Aisling wasn't backing down.

"I said, that, ah . . ." Mears cracked. He knew that he couldn't fire Aisling under the Labor-negotiated contract that Montgomery County teachers had, unless she were sleeping with one of her minor students *and* letting such a relationship influence her grading. "I just think, that . . . ah," he continued. "I think that you should read his work again and reconsider your interim grade."

"Reconsider *what*? He didn't turn in half his work! I don't care if his father is president of the world; it has nothing to do with my judging his son's work."

Mears cleared his throat. "Well, would you at least look at what he did turn in, and if you still think it warrants an interim notice, then so be it."

Aisling lifted a small stack of papers and scanned them for five minutes; then she turned to the department chair and said, "I stand by my decision."

Mears forced a smile.

"Mr O'Meara, Mr O'Meara?" My parent had arrived. It was my turn to take center stage.

The next week changed my life.

It was clear to me that if I was to do any financial maneuvering like Vic had suggested, I had to get my money back in my hands and out of Bernie's. I took the morning off and mustered all I had to prepare for battle.

After all, those certificates belonged to *me*. They didn't belong to Bernie. I had paid for them. I should be able to keep them wherever I damn well pleased! I laughed to think of how bold I had felt by merely photocopying them. Photocopies meant nothing. I wanted the originals. They belonged to me. And I would not let Bernie stand in my way of getting them.

"Fine. Take them," Bernie said later when I confronted him.

I was surprised on two counts: One, Bernie was suddenly so easily available, and two, he was so easily acceding. (Little did I know at the time that Capital Ventures was rapidly deteriorating. The whole corporate structure was falling apart.)

Next, I had to retrieve my banker's fund and money market account. To do this, I had to make a trip to Old Republic. The branch I went to looked like a savings and loan out of the 1950s. There were four tellers behind heavy metal bars that were reinforced with Plexiglas. In the center of the room was a rectangular oak table with various forms in little boxes in the middle and some old ballpoint pens attached to silver colored chains that, in turn, were anchored in the wood.

I got in line behind cage number one. The teller was a slight man wearing a shirt whose collar was too big for him. He also had on a ready-made red tie with black slanted stripes.

"There's going to be a penalty for early withdrawal," said the little man as he adjusted his big glasses.

"I want my money."

"Well, this is a rather large amount. I'll have to get my supervisor." I didn't like the sound of this. But I came prepared with the name of the investment manager at Riggs Bank at the corner of M Street and Wisconsin Avenue in Georgetown. He gave me a wire number for transfer. He was also an important person in the banking community. They wouldn't dare mess with him.

For once I was right. Though it took over an hour, I had the money transferred from both the banker's fund and the money market into an account at Riggs. I was on a roll. Now, I had my securities from Capital Ventures and some real money.

Third, I had to get Mookie. He owed me. It would be Mookie who would stiff the bank. I figured it was more his line than mine. I called him up and explained what the deal would be.

Mookie was in and came right over.

"Let me see if I got this. You got some paper from Capital Ventures and you want me to stink out on a bank loan at Old Republic?"

I nodded.

Mookie got up and walked over to the window. I wondered if he was still being watched. Maybe people like Mookie were always being followed. He lifted the sheer drape slightly to get a better view. Then, while continuing to look out, he said, "You say you got a life insurance inheritance?"

"That's where it all began."

"You know I could have made some money for you."

"Uh-huh." I didn't want to insult him, but I hardly classed him in the league with Salomon Brothers.

Mookie looked back to me. "I know you don't believe me, but it's true. If you've got money, you can make more. No problem."

I nodded. It was time to cut to the chase. "Will you do it?"

"How much money are we talking about?"

I hesitated.

Mookie understood my hesitancy immediately. "Hey, you called me. I didn't call you."

He was right. Either I went with him or I didn't. "I've got four hundred thousand in paper. I understand I can get eighty percent on this, so I'm expecting three hundred-twenty thousand back."

"Shit man! You've got that kind of money? Man, did I have you pegged wrong. And you're living like this?" He motioned to my shabby dwelling as if I were the biggest idiot in the world. "I don't get it. If I had that kind of money I would spend it. You only go around once, you know."

"Are you going to help me or not?"

"What's in it for me?"

"Mookie! You owe me. You wrecked my car. My only car."

"That car wasn't worth five hundred dollars."

"It was all I had."

"How about I give you five hundred dollars and take a split on this?"

"Everyone's got their hands in my pocket," I said. Now it was my turn to feel that I'd misjudged *my* neighbor.

Mookie bounced over and sat on the arm of the couch. "Look, on the open market this stuff isn't tradable. You've got nothing here but a big pile of toilet paper. Old Republic isn't going to give you eighty percent on this. Try five or ten percent."

I started to protest, but Mookie put his hand on my arm.

"Now, I think I know some people who would pay top dollar for your worthless paper."

"What kind of people?"

"The kind of people who'd like to see Capital Ventures out of business. The kind of people who could use this as a lever, a mark – do you follow?"

I nodded – even though I didn't follow.

"What I'm saying is this: I'll try to get you sixty, seventy, or eighty percent – whatever I can from people who *are* interested in buying this stuff. And if I do, any excess I get I'll keep as my commission. Is that fair?"

Was that fair? What did I have to lose? Right now all I had was the remainder of my banker's fund and money market money, about five hundred-forty thousand. We shook hands on it. Right or wrong, at least I was doing *something*.

12 St Georges Avenue
London, N7
January 12, 1991

Dear Michael,

I've made some original observations on the Valediction poems. I still have tons of secondary work to do, but I now believe that Donne's Valediction poems are connected by the Aristotelian notion of the four causes. There are four poems and four causes. It all fits perfectly. I'll enclose a draft abstract as soon as I complete it.

Hugh says the significance of my discovery may force others both to re-examine the way Donne is normally read (with a tie between the early poems and the religious work) and to highlight the way Aristotle was understood in the early seventeenth century. It is widely believed that the seventeenth century eschewed Aristotle (due to the revolutions in science). This work may refute such an extreme view.

I find myself lost in my work. It is totally consuming. There is such an intensity with original research. I feel as if I am unlocking the doors of Truth. The whole thing seems so important that I feel humbled to be the one called upon to do it. Hugh says I may get an offer as an assistant lecturer at King's College next fall. That may not mean much to you, but it is extremely rare for anyone to get assistant lectureships in the Humanities these days – and for an American in Britain, it is virtually unheard of!

I must tell you my head is upside down. I look to Hugh for my basic direction. We are seeing a lot of each other. The man has aided my work immeasurably. He is so unselfish. Well, I could go on, but I've got to fit this on my aerogramme form.

All the best,
Aisling

Well.

That was either a "Dear John" letter or the emanations of one overly active scholar. Out of sight, out of mind – and I'm going out of mine!

"Oh don't worry, Michael. It won't be bad," Ash had told me when she'd first gotten the letter from the Women's Education Fund accepting her for a doctoral fellowship. The program was for women who had had their careers interrupted and wanted to go back to school.

This worried me.

But I couldn't stop her. Her doctorate had already been put on hold twice. She had begun it at Penn (a good school in English literature), but the timing was bad. She'd worked too intensely, and then dropped out after two years. Five years later, she enrolled at the University of Maryland and finished her course work, passed her prelims, and started doing research. But again there was a problem. She began "losing her direction" (her words, not mine). She felt it was time to step back from academic research and get into pure teaching. After a temporary stint at a private school, she came upon the permanent job opening at Fairview – and presto!

She arrived at Fairview shortly after I had split with Sara (but before the final divorce had been granted). I admired her otherworldliness. She rarely saw things in a practical way. No. Aisling was an idealist who wanted reality to be as she envisioned it.

We began dating and "got serious" shortly thereafter. Unlike Sara, Ash didn't try to "remake me." She didn't view herself as Pygmalion. Every disagreement with Sara had been a confrontation about power: her will against mine. And since my will wasn't overly strong, I generally lost. If Sara hadn't moved in with Buddy, I doubt I'd ever have gotten divorced.

"So where will you get your degree?" I asked her when she received the acceptance letter. "University of London or Maryland?"

"The Women's Education Fund doesn't stipulate." She was too excited to sit down. She held the letter in her hand and paced back and forth. "But I suppose it's up to me where my degree is issued."

"If it were me, I'd decide that in a hurry."

Was I hoping she'd choose to stay in the States? You betcha. It is not the most heartening thing to see the woman you love (but aren't married to) declare suddenly that she's leaving the country on an "extended stay."

"Ten months. A year at the most. I'll be back. You'll see, Michael. I'll be back."

I got in the car to drive away from Washington. Not in my car. I was without wheels. I borrowed Angie's car.

I wasn't leaving for good. Just taking a trip. A day trip to New York City to take in a musical with Angie. *Les Misérables*. I'd read the book. Twice. I wondered how Jean Valjean would be transformed onstage. The evil Javert – was he really evil or a man who took justice to an extreme? Was there some sort of line that one passed in the continuum of Goodness? Up to that line, you are good. Past that line, you are bad. All the time you are moving in the same direction. The downfall of zealots.

> The quality of mercy is not strained;
> It droppeth as the gentle rain from heaven
> Upon the place beneath. It is twice blest;
> It blesseth him that gives and him that takes.

The Bishop of D___ changed Jean Valjean. I wondered what was changing me?

The five-hour drive to New York, up the New Jersey Turnpike to the George Washington Bridge, allows one time to think. Angie and I talked of Fairview and how we had gotten there.

"I don't think anyone can be a high school teacher all her life," Angie said. "It's too draining. If you do it right you die a little every year." Who sighs most hastens the other's death. The anima drains right out of you. I wondered if that had happened to Aisling. No, not that.

"What do you plan to do after teaching, then?" I asked her.

"After teaching? Who knows? Maybe I can start a . . . family."

I nodded.

"I believe children are better raised when the mother is at home."

I nodded.

"I'd like to raise some children and then, perhaps, do something else, like writing."

I nodded. I waited. Traffic on the George Washington Bridge was always terribly slow.

The city. We parked in an all-day garage and took to the street. It was noon and the matinee started at one thirty. It was time for lunch. What better than Rockefeller Center? Our maitre d'hotel fished into his silver cart and handed me a hot pretzel. Angie took a Polish hot dog with relish oozing at the seams.

We found a spot to sit and watched humanity pass by. No one really cared whether we were there or not, whether we lived or died. We could have been in the middle of the forest. In one way it would have been the same. Trees don't give a damn, either.

After the musical, Angie and I walked to Carnegie Deli for dinner. Corned beef. Cream soda. And don't forget the cheesecake.

"I am happy," Angie said as we lingered over our coffee.

"What did you enjoy most? The play, the city, the dinner?"

"Everything."

Angie gave me a look I'd seen before. Her hair seemed to bounce.

"I guess we've had a complete day," I said.

"Not quite complete," was her reply. Then she opened her purse and handed me a letter. I opened it. It was a confirmation of reservations at the Hilton New York on the Avenue of the Americas.

"You've thought of everything," was all I could manage.

"Don't thank me. Daddy got these and couldn't use them. Ergo, here we are."

How convenient, I thought, as Angie reached out and took my hand.

Chapter Eight

I came back from New York City and found Mookie sitting at my kitchen table eating a TV dinner.

"Hey, man. You should get better shit to eat around here. This stuff tastes like cardboard."

I walked over to the Formica table and pulled the foil tray toward me. "Don't eat it if it tastes like cardboard."

Mookie took the tray back. "I'm hungry. You sure took your time in coming home. It built up my appetite just waiting here." He shoveled in the turkey and mashed potatoes. Four movements of the jaw, and the stuff was headed for his stomach. "Gourmet Delight. Next time you go to the store, buy Gourmet Delight."

"I'll keep that in mind," I replied.

He finished the food in two more mega-mouthfuls, washed it down with soda, burped, and then was ready to talk. The only problem was, I *wasn't*.

"I think I've got someone to do the deed, but I can't give you your money back on that paper for a while. Don't worry. I'll make you whole. Maybe a few months. I don't know. You don't think I could pry a little more out of you? I've got another deal . . ."

"Nice talking with you, Mookie." But what alternative did I have? The four hundred thousand was probably lost. No sense jumping all over Mookie about it. I had made the mistake of trusting Bernie. If Mookie could retrieve any of it, then so much the better. What did I have to lose? It was already lost. But the five hundred and forty thousand (the balance of money that I'd retrieved from Old Republic minus the penalties) was now safely in a rolling certificate of deposits at Riggs Bank, a federally insured bank that was as respectable as they come. I wasn't going to touch *that* money until they sent me the income checks – income checks came from 85 percent of the interest generated. That money would be mine to live off while the balance was rolled over along with 15 percent of the interest into the next six-month period. Gradually, the principal would grow. And there were no service fees. It wasn't a bonanza, but it was probably the only money I'd ever see from the inheritance.

I ushered Mookie out of the apartment. "Don't screw me, Mookie," I said in my sternest tone. I may have kissed off that money, but he didn't know it.

He smiled. "Hey man. Don't worry. I won't screw you – you're not my type."

Winter is not my favorite season. My supplementary stipend for coaching cross-country and track is temporarily interrupted then. I would have to wait until April 15 for my pay to bounce back up again. In the meantime, I was loaded with money but didn't have access to a penny of it. The bills continued to arrive. In fact, they increased; the thought of having money had stimulated my spending habits. I was merely paying the interest on my credit card (which I had foolishly extended due to my great expectations). I had no car. I had no clear direction in life. Aisling had dear-johned me. But I did have Angie, and that worried me. Everything was mixed up.

It was Saturday at the hardware store. I could get in ten hours on a Saturday. That was seventy-five dollars. I could use the cash flow.

Ours was an old-fashioned hardware store, the kind that sold nails and washers individually by weight. We scooped them out of trays, put them onto the old metal scale, calculated the price, and then dumped them into little brown paper bags on which we wrote the price with a marking pen.

We had modern packaging, too, on some items, but that's not what drew customers to our store. What we provided was the personal touch. A listening ear. Kind of like my free period at school. The hardware customers came in wanting to fix a faucet or caulk a tub, but we ended up talking about the lot of being a struggling homeowner. I gave advice, nodded my head as I weighted out the nuts.

It always seemed appropriate that Lent came in the winter. Lent is a time of reflection and self-denial. In winter, self-denial was a way of life. No more trips to New York. No fancy plays. Only videos with Angie or books from the library.

On Sunday I went to the soup kitchen. This was a place I had often gone to in the past, when I had nowhere to turn. The kitchen was a cooperative effort. At around ten o'clock, five hundred tickets are given out to the people waiting outside. The tickets had a "1" or a "2" printed on them, which referred to the first or the second seating. Mothers with children were given priority. Meanwhile, in the kitchen, we were frying chicken, making mashed potatoes, gravy, beans, and tea. When everything was ready, we served the food on paper plates and loaded the plates onto trays. A couple of pieces of white bread on top kept everything secure. The trays were stacked in slotted stainless-steel carts that carried fifteen trays at a time. Then the carts were wheeled out and the people were served.

Some of the volunteers were models of efficiency. Not me. I tended to chat it up a bit with the men and women I served. There was always quite a diverse group of people being served, but they had one thing in common: they were hungry and needed a good meal.

"Lost my job at the candy factory."

"Daddy's not never coming back."

"This is a leg. I don't like legs. Can't you give me another piece?"

One man I served wore a blank expression, as if he were in another world. His fingers were stained yellow. His body smelled vile. "Here's your dinner," I said to him.

The man touched my arm. "My father died."

"I'm sorry," I replied.

"My father died."

"When did it happen?" I asked, thinking he might need help with the funeral arrangements.

"When I went away. I went away, and he died." The man was now looking directly into my eyes.

"You went away?"

"I had to go away. The government made me."

I nodded my head. I had to serve another meal, but the man would not let go of my arm.

"Nineteen sixty-eight. Vietnam. I went away. They made me. And now my father's dead."

I touched his hand, and he loosened his grip. His gaze was distant again.

Somehow I made it through Lent.

It was March 30. Tomorrow was Easter Sunday. The spring was coming. The country was high on its military operation in the Persian Gulf. The president was strutting about, and there was a lot of talk among the students about "kicking ass."

The signup sheet for the track team was posted, and a positive feeling was rising among most everyone. I was at church helping Father Mac set up extra chairs for the Midnight Mass. Easter is a big day in Christian churches. Extra services. Large plate offerings. The trouble from a priest's point of view is that it comes at the end of Holy Week, which is also full of extra services. In addition, there is the all-night vigil. People were scurrying about decorating the sanctuary. The somber Lenten colors and atmosphere had to be transformed to the vital beauty of life.

Somehow, I felt a bit out of sync. Instead of Christian religious lyrics, my mind recalled Yeats:

> Too long a sacrifice
> Can make a stone of the heart.
> O when may it suffice?
> That is Heaven's part, our part
> To murmur name upon name
> As a mother names her child
> When sleep at last has come
> On limbs that had run wild.
> What is it but nightfall?
> No, no, not night but death

I went home and skipped Easter. I was not ready for it.

A Story of Aisling – Part Three

The third time I saw Aisling was at the Humanities faculty Christmas party. It was held at the Kenwood Country Club. One of the English Department spouses was a big-time lawyer and was on the club's board. Hence, we had many school functions there.

Kenwood wasn't Congressional or Avenel. *Those* country clubs were cutting edge: fifty to seventy-five thousand initial membership fee and that didn't include the monthly dues. Kenwood was 25 percent cheaper, but there was a catch. You had to be of the right sort in order for them to accept your money. It was the bastion of "old money." Nobody on the faculty at Fairview could (on the basis of their Fairview salary) afford to buy even a hoagie in the clubroom, much less to mix with these fixtures of affluence.

But there were those on the faculty who took teaching high school at Fairview to be merely a diversion, who didn't really need the money. These were the men or women married to the real moneymakers: the politicians, the diplomats, the heart surgeons, the bankers, the corporate lawyers, *ad nauseam*. There is a division of economic classes at Fairview: the "haves" (who teach to keep themselves occupied) and the "have-nots" (who actually pay their bills from the money they earn). At the Humanities party held at the country club, the two groups were neatly segregated. There was no rule about this, but the result was the same as if there had been.

I was with the latter group, freshening up my drink, when I bumped into Aisling.

"Oh, I'm sorry," I said as I spilled eggnog on her dress. It was the same sort of dress that she wore to school. (That's another distinction between the haves and the have-nots: the gentry step up their attire for occasions such as this.)

She smiled. "My name's Aisling," she said, pronouncing the name "Ash-ling" and extending her hand.

I took her hand and shook it. I was so disoriented that I couldn't respond.

Aisling helped me out, "And you are Michael O'Meara." I nodded dumbly.

"Do you like this party?"

I shook my head.

"Do you want to get out of here?"

I nodded my head.

"Do you have a car?"

I nodded again.

"Well, then. Just follow me. We'll have a Christmas party that will beat the pants off this one."

There was something about the way she talked . . . I followed her away from the haves and have-nots.

It was December in Washington, DC. This meant that the weather was in the high forties and there was no snow on the ground. I drove my car, following Aisling in hers to a little Italian restaurant just off Dupont Circle. We had to park in a lot because the on-street parking was nonexistent.

"Sorry about the lot," Aisling said, climbing out of her car, "but I thought we'd never find parking near each other. She smiled. It was a funny kind of smile, beginning on one side of her face and twitching upward. The only way that you could tell it was a smile was from the twinkle in Aisling's blue Irish eyes.

Then she jerked her head and led me to the restaurant, Papa Giovanni's, a very small restaurant located just off an alley. In another era, I might have thought I was being led into a private speakeasy. I wondered if there'd be a free table, it being Saturday night at nine o'clock. But, apparently, Papa Giovanni's is not an overly frequented restaurant. I could see part of the reason why immediately. First, there was only a small wooden sign above the door that signified its existence. Second, the street number was 1609½ – hardly the most prestigious of addresses. Third, you had to ring a buzzer just to get someone to come to the door and let you in.

This devotion to anonymity certainly cut down on street traffic.

When we rang, we had to wait almost two minutes until someone answered. I was very anxious. "Maybe they're closed," I offered. Again the smile. More dead time. "Maybe –" Aisling put her fingers on my arm. Lightly. I looked up. I felt stupid. But she wasn't judging me. I was judging myself.

Then a man of about thirty answered the door. "Prego," he said. He was of medium build with strong muscles in his neck and shoulders. His vibrant black hair was not fully combed. I immediately liked him.

"I'm ready for my dinner," Aisling said.

"So I see. You have a friend," he said nodding to me.

"Yes."

"Then come in."

The entranceway to the place was a long hallway that was very dark and smelled of something that I couldn't describe, but it was a mildly pleasant scent that spoke of age. When we turned the corner we came upon a small room that was dimly lit and contained only four tables that could be square or circular depending upon whether four leaves on hinges were snapped up or down. When the leaves were down the tables were square and sat one to four, and when the leaves were snapped up the tables became circular and could sit up to eight, I reckoned. Two tables were occupied. We were escorted to the back right table and seated at one of the unoccupied tables made up as a square. In front of us at another table (set up as a circle) was a family of five – a husband and wife along with their teenage daughter, preteen son, and the little boy who was no doubt the gift of their older years.

At the other table (set up as a square) were two immaculately dressed Korean men deep in conversation. The older man (around fifty-five) was doing most of the talking. The younger man (around twenty-five) was the listener, though, from time to time, he would make a point that occasioned a period of silence.

The man who had seated us disappeared and was replaced by an older man (around seventy), who presented us with two menus. "And how are you tonight, Aisling?"

"I'm well, Papa Giovanni."

"Good. I am so happy you have arrived to take your dinner."

Then I saw another Aisling smile. It was a full smile that showed her teeth and made her whole visage vibrant.

We took up our menus, and I realized that I was in the wrong restaurant. "Say, Aisling. These prices are pretty steep. I don't think that I can afford to –"

"That's not a problem."

"Well, maybe not for you, but for me it's fantasy land."

"It's not a problem for either of us. This meal is on the house."

"Are you serious?"

"Yes, you see last year, I taught at Sidwell Friends School, in a leave-replacement position when things were going badly for me in my PhD program at Maryland. It was for only one year. Papa Giovanni's granddaughter was a student who was having a hard time, so I gave her some extra help, and by the end of the year she got an A in English. The family was so grateful for what I'd done for their granddaughter that they offered to give me a complimentary dinner for two. It's been about six months since then, but I decided to call in the chip tonight. Merry Christmas."

I didn't know what to say. This was four or five times more expensive than any restaurant that I had ever eaten at in my life. Aisling seemed to take it all in stride.

"Have you ever eaten at this kind of place before?" I asked.

"If you mean, have I ever eaten at a place this expensive before, then the answer is no. But I think we should forget about all of that. It will ruin the experience. Just think of this as the Alternate Humanities Christmas Party."

I liked that. Somehow it made sense. Christmas was a time of celebration. Here we were, opening Aisling's gift. And she was sharing it with me.

On the walls of Papa Giovanni's were many pictures of the family on various vacations. Each was framed in a cheap black wood frame with glass to protect the photo.

Aisling and I began to scan the pictures. "I bet that's Filippo," she ventured.

"Filippo?"

"The son who escorted us inside. It was his daughter who I helped. He has a day job and does this only to help out his parents."

"That's a lot of work," I said.

"Well, they're open only on the weekends these days. They've had this restaurant for years. Actually, they own a minority share of this entire building. Got into it years ago from a grateful and loyal client who gave them a 'ground-floor' opportunity. I would guess that the only reason they continue with the restaurant is out of love."

"Love?"

"When you're excellent at something, you can't just give it up."

I nodded. The Korean men were being served a fruit and cheese dessert along with fluted glasses of almond-colored wine. At the other table, the little boy was beginning to make a fuss. Papa Giovanni looked out from the kitchen and then his head disappeared. In a couple of minutes, he brought out a brightly colored plate with some pasta that was shaped like bow ties surrounded by little cylinders filled with something green. In his other hand he had a special little flower.

"The specialty of the house," he said with a flourish as he approached the family's round table. The little boy looked up at his gift with pride. He made no more noise.

"I think I like Papa Giovanni," I said to Aisling. I put my hands into my sport coat pockets, as was my custom when I wanted to emphasize a point – and out popped a paperback book onto the floor. "Sorry," I said as I bent down to pick it up.

"What are you reading?"

"Well, I'm not actually reading it, really. You see I'm teaching Modern European History and there's a section on World War Two and the various US citizens who made broadcasts for the enemy. One of them was Ezra Pound. I thought I'd try to glance at some of his poems to try to get an understanding about why he did it."

"It's not on the approved curriculum," she chided.

"Please don't turn me in."

"Let me see that book while I decide," she said. I handed her the book. She turned to the table of contents and then handed it back to me. "Wrong book."

"What?"

"Wrong book. This is a selection of Pound's early work. Mostly from *Personae*. You need a version of the *Cantos*. *The Pisan Cantos* will be best – particularly the passages on 'usury.'"

I nodded. I really wasn't sure what usury had to do with it.

"You see Pound had a theory that usury corrupted the financial system and was heading Western civilization in the wrong direction. You can read about it in Kenner's book on Pound."

I took out a scrap of paper and wrote everything down.

"Thank you," I said. "I appreciate it."

Michael Boylan

"And *I* appreciate talking to a Fairview teacher who actually *cares* about what he's teaching enough to read some poems by Ezra Pound in order to make better sense of something."

I felt my face flush. I turned and saw the Koreans finishing their dessert. Their time was soon ending, while ours was just beginning.

On Monday, April 1, I found myself the butt of several pranks. During second period, my lectern was missing. It was found in Maggie Johnson's math class along with three others. Then, at fourth period, the entire class was absent save for Martha Sinclair (a very quiet girl).

"Do you know where the class is?" I asked her.

"I don't know," she replied without looking at me. "But I heard something about the cafeteria."

I nodded. Either Martha was in on it or she wasn't. I wasn't going to hold class just for her, so I hiked over to the cafeteria. There was nobody there except our principal, Imogene Porton. Ms Porton had the nickname "Imagines she's important" or "Ms Im-portant" for short. The name fit.

"Did you lose something, Michael?"

"My class," I replied.

"What would your class be doing in the cafeteria?"

"I don't know."

"I suggest that your classroom would be more appropriate. No snacking before lunch!" she said through her parental smile. Her teeth had recently been bonded so that her naturally gray enamel was now an Ultrabrite toothpaste commercial.

I nodded and headed back.

Martha was in on it. Sure enough, when I returned to the class-room, I found the students all in their seats with a look of general impatience. At least I had my lectern.

Even the teachers were playing jokes on each other. I decided it was best to hurry home at the final bell.

I was working out the schedules for track when I heard a knock on the door. It was Mookie. I hadn't seen him in over a month.

"Since when do you knock, Mookie?"

"Hey Michael, my man. My main man. Mookie's got a surprise for you."

"What is it, a whoopie cushion? I've had my fill of jokes today."

"No joke, man," he said, taking out a key ring and handing it to me.

"What's this?"

"A key ring."

I frowned.

"Let's go outside and see." There was a sly smile on his face.

We went down to the parking lot. A dark blue BMW was parked in the space where I used to park my Pontiac. I looked over at Mookie.

"Try the key," he said.

I did. The door unlocked. I got in behind the wheel. Mookie got in on the passenger side.

"What do you think?"

"It's a nice car you bought, Mookie. What are you going to do with your Celica?"

"Not my car. Your car," Mookie replied.

"What?"

"Your car. Your very own."

"Is this some kind of joke? I can't afford –"

"It's not perfectly new. It's got fifteen thousand miles on it. Repossessed by someone I know. A real *steal*."

I wondered how literally I should take the terms "steal" and "repossessed." He was serious. This was no April Fools' joke. But how could I afford the upkeep? The insurance?

"Kind of takes you, don't it?"

I nodded my head.

"Now, for some extra expenses you might have, unlock the glove compartment."

I did. It was stuffed with new bills still in their wrappers. I took one packet out. They were hundreds.

"Twenty thousand. Cash. Just to pick up your spirits."

"What is this, Mookie? Where did you –"

"What you don't know won't hurt you. Let's just say your money has been working. Call this a first installment. One car worth 20K and 20K in currency. New bills. Just printed this morning."

I looked again at the money.

"No man." Mookie laughed. "Not counterfeit. I'd never do that to my main man. No way. I've got all your paperwork in my pocket here. Time to go for a spin."

I did what I was told. I had almost a year's salary in the glove compartment. My first stop was a fancy fish restaurant on Wisconsin. My second stop was the hardware store, where I quit.

No more nuts for me.

Chapter Nine

Things were looking up. Mookie stopped by every so often and dropped off suits, jewelry, and cash. I liked the cash. It felt good. I began a personal custom of always traveling with a thousand dollars in "C-notes" on me. I mean, really, what's a thousand dollars to a millionaire?

It was strange. When I *actually* had my million I still felt poor. Now that I had lost almost half of my inheritance and had turned collections over to Mookie, I felt rich. I was living off the fat. I liked that.

Everyone began treating me differently. To Vic Santini, I was no longer a poor schmuck but a savvy character.

"You're lucky you got your money out of Capital Ventures when you did, Michael. That whole operation is falling apart, quick. Old Republic is being investigated by the RTC, and Schmidt Properties just declared bankruptcy."

"Oh yeah?"

"Look, it's in today's paper." Vic slid the *Washington Post* over my way.

Amid investigations and alleged scandal, Schmidt Properties filed for bankruptcy today, thus ending several days of speculation on the fate of the one-time real estate empire. Schmidt Properties began to experience troubles when the commercial market tightened last year. However, the contraction of residential properties proved to be Schmidt's downfall. Yesterday, it was reported that there may have been some improprieties in the way funds were accounted. States Attorney Richard Cohen said in a statement to the press, "It appears to be a Ponzi fraud with new monies used to cover old debts. This only works when the market is expanding. In our present economic condition there was no way they could continue." Prosecutor Cohen went on to say that they expected several indictments in the next few days. Unnamed sources in the prosecutor's office say that indictments are imminent on Schmidt president Klaus von Grossman and his top aides. M. William Tweed, a company spokesman, said that his firm had no comment.

I did a double take. M. William Tweed. Rhymes with "greed." That was the slob who had tried to put the screws on me about Sara. I wondered how he had been designated "company spokesman," unless the rest of those poor bastards were heading south.

I couldn't resist calling my ex-wife. Unfortunately, it was a man who answered the phone.

"I want Sara."

"Why? Who are you?"

"Let's just say I'm an interested party."

"Why won't you Schmidt assholes leave us alone? I already told you everything is in Sara's name. I own nothing except the shirt on my back. My wife's got it all. Understand?"

I wasn't sure I did. "Everything is in your wife, Sara's, name?"

"What's wrong, is there an echo on this line? I already told you. Now leave us alone. You're not going to get a cent!"

Then there was dial tone.

I had to check this out and I did. It wasn't long before I had verified facts:

1 Buddy Braegan used to work with Schmidt properties.
2 Schmidt was after Buddy for monies Buddy owed them.

3   Buddy needed an out.
4   Buddy transferred his assets to his wife's name.
5   His wife's name was Sara.

So Sara had gotten married. Number three. The charm. It was a charm for me. No more alimony. I wondered why she had never told me. Well, I didn't *really* wonder.

This called for a celebration. I was going out with Angie, anyway. Now we'd make it a night on the town. I'd take Angie places I used to go with Sara. It seemed like cosmic justice. My karma had definitely turned.

A Story About Angie

It all happened in one day. She had long awaited the event, but for it to happen in one day was against the odds. She felt that fate must be on her side. Which letter should she open first? Brown, the University of Maryland, or St Mary's? Brown was her first choice. The crimson letterhead always attracted her with its simple elegance. She would be so happy if she could get in. Her mother had taken a job for the express purpose of funding her daughter's college. They'd have been pressed if Angie's brother, Marty, had chosen college, too. They had wanted Marty *to want* college, but instead he picked the navy.

Now, there was only Angie. Her mother's salary could put her into Brown.

"It's just like those contests," Vic said when she had filled out the applications. "If you tell them you're buying one of their magazines, you get put onto one pile. If you check 'No,' you get put on the shit pile."

Therefore, Angie did not apply for financial aid. She wanted Brown to know that she was a full-paying applicant. Brown could turn a profit on full-paying students. And everybody wanted to turn a profit. "It's the American way," her dad used to say.

No one was home. For a brief moment Angie considered whether she should wait to open the letter. Her parents would want to share her joy. But they would not be home for another hour.

She decided to make herself comfortable on the couch in the living room. Once seated, she pushed under the envelope flap with one finger. It was tightly glued. She pressed harder. Her finger turned, and she got a paper cut. Instinctively, she squeezed it and a drop of blood appeared. It was no matter. She didn't even pause. This time the envelope not only opened but ripped almost in half. Fortunately, the letter was safe. She unfolded the paper. "Thank you for applying to Brown University. . . . Many outstanding applicants . . . More than we can accept. . . ."

She opened the next letter. "Regret to inform you . . ."

She tossed the third to the floor unopened. The plate glass was all that stood between her and the ravine that was their backyard. She knew that her parents would be proud that she would be going to St Mary's. They would never betray any sadness or disappointment over this. In fact, Vic would tell everyone that St Mary's was the best little school in the country. Not well known. A real sleeper. Highly underrated except by those in the know, of course.

Outside, a male cardinal was perched on a branch. It would be only a moment before that cardinal flew away. She waited for that moment.

But the bird lingered even as the drop of blood from the paper cut fell upon her letter from Brown.

"What do you mean, a house?" I asked as Mookie was prancing about.

"Yeah man. No time to chat. Got to move. Got to move."

So we moved. We drove up River Road to Potomac, where many expensive new 7,500-square-foot houses stood. Mookie drove the BMW. I stared out the window at the landscape. Spreading before me was big money. New money. Garish money.

When I stepped out of the car I was puzzled. Before me was a behemoth. Three levels. Pink-colored brick. A four-car garage.

"Hey, what do you think? Wait till you see inside!"

We entered. It was just like the set of a movie. Was this real or ersatz? I didn't know the difference. All I knew was that I felt a longing to become "squire of the manor." Was I fit to become "squire of the manor"?

"Hey, you know, they've overbuilt these things, and this one went down with Schmidt Properties."

"You mean it's ours? Mine?"

"Ours. For a while at any rate. We don't own it, but we can live here rent-free. All we have to pay are the utilities. We've even got a maid. Maria's her name. Doesn't speak much English."

"What's the catch?"

"No catch. A kind of 'thank you' for what you did to Capital Ventures."

"What *did* I do to Capital Ventures?"

Mookie only laughed. It was time to move up to another station in life. I looked. I came. I moved in.

Part Two

Chapter Ten

It was May in Washington. My favorite month of the year. The azaleas were in full bloom, as were the dogwoods. The entire landscape was a fairyland. I liked to go on runs through the surrounding neighborhoods and feel enveloped by the beauty of it all. I have always been convinced that aesthetic beauty is one of the ways we can think of the larger picture: of history, for example. When I run through vibrant whites, pinks, violets, and reds, I am transported to a different level of awareness. No longer do I think about current events, but am instead propelled into contemplation of the grand changes that have characterized the ebb and flow of this century. What themes have moved us? Idealism may have motivated some Communists and Fascists, but their actual policies were so evil as to make a mockery of anyone who found any abstract justification in their founding principles.

And counter reactions can become as bad as the forces they were opposing. Joseph McCarthy could be applauded for opposing Communism, but he was a zealot who lost sight of common decency as he engaged in his tactics of intimidation and innuendo.

Then there was the civil rights movement.

For some reason people (as a group) feel the need to analyze and characterize their own kind. This classification identity scheme is connected with judgments about one's ultimate worth.

The basic way of humankind in history has been to hurt and punish those who are different.

All this occasioned by the beauty of spring!

A Story of Aisling – Part Four

Aisling loved spring as well. On April 1 we had gone down to the Tidal Basin for a walk to view the cherry blossoms, an annual event in Washington. The annual event is jammed with people for a week when the fragile white and faintly rose-colored flowers hesitantly bloom, display themselves, and then fall away.

Aisling and I walked around the entire Tidal Basin. We had gotten there rather early in order to avoid the crowds. (Or so we thought.) But it was such a good idea that everyone else had done the same.

I loved looking at the black boughs and their delicate pink petals.

"I wish I'd brought my camera," I said to Aisling.

"Beauty does long to be captured," she replied.

"Yes. I mean just look over there. If you knelt down and shot upward toward the sunrise, wouldn't that be beautiful?"

"I'm not sure you're supposed to shoot into the sun, Michael."

"Oh, you can do it if you have the proper equipment."

"Perhaps you can do anything if you have the proper equipment."

I gave her a hug.

Just after crossing the bridge, we made the turn toward the Jefferson Memorial, walking across a perfect picnic ground on an upward slope of land choked with trees. A group of women there caught my eye.

On a blanket, four women in their early thirties reclined near an architectural model. Working blueprints were stretched out around them. Their breakfast was a big bowl of strawberries, some heavy cream, and a case of champagne (three bottles of which had already been consumed). One of the women was dipping a strawberry into the cream while another had her head tilted back to taste the delightful treat. As she chomped down on the strawberry, her left foot shifted to the right and knocked over the model.

At this, all the women laughed *very* loudly.

"I'm glad I won't be living in their building," I said. Aisling merely laughed.

Next we came upon some children who were climbing one of the cherry trees and pulling blossoms off in hunks. We looked around for their parents, but saw none (apart from the crush of people taking the same walk we were).

Aisling walked up to the children. "Now you don't want to be doing that. Those blossoms are for everyone. When you pull off whole branches of them, then there's less for everyone." The children stopped what they were doing.

Then, suddenly, a smallish man of about forty-five with a balding pate and about fifty pounds too much around his belly came running toward us. A woman about fifteen years his junior and perfectly proportioned came up behind. The man was dressed in a business suit and the woman was also nattily attired for work. "What are you doing?" the man yelled at Aisling.

Aisling turned and confronted him. "Your children were pulling branches off the cherry tree. I was telling them not to do it."

"What right have you to talk to *my* children?" asked the man.

"Yes, you bitch. What are you doing? I have half a mind to call the cops," his wife chimed in.

Aisling didn't know to whom she should respond. She looked to the man and then to the woman. "Yes, why don't you call the police? Then you can explain to them how those branches got on the ground and how your children happen to have their hands full of others. As you can see from the ubiquitous signs, each act of defacing these trees is punishable by a three-hundred-dollar fine. By the look of things, you'll owe the District of Columbia more than two thousand dollars."

"Why, you bitch!" the woman screamed as she lunged at Aisling.

I interceded and stopped the woman. "I'm just a bystander," I said. "What this lady has been saying is entirely correct. Don't add assault to your crime. I'm a witness to everything."

They must have been lawyers because they instantly folded and rounded up their brood for a fast retreat.

"The bigger they are, the harder they fall," I said.

"The bigger they are, the stupider they are," Aisling responded.

By then we were at the Jefferson Memorial. It is really an impressive site in the early morning with the Tidal Basin in front of it decked out in all its finery.

Aisling and I stood on the steps of the memorial. "There's an art show I want to see," she said. "A Turner show. I've always liked Turner. It's at the Philadelphia Art Museum."

"And it's not coming to Washington?"

"No. LA, Chicago, and Philadelphia."

"Okay. When is it?"

"Next month."

"Can we drive up and back in a day?"

"We could, but I don't want to."

"Well, you know a motel room is pretty expensive. My money is kind of tight just now – but I could pick up some extra cash working at the hardware store."

"No, Michael. I don't want you to work extra hours at the hardware store. I think that you shouldn't have to work *any* hours at the hardware store. Look, I used to live in Philadelphia. I started my PhD at the University of Pennsylvania."

"Started? What happened? Why didn't you stay?"

"That's another story. What I mean is, I have a friend, Grace, who has a large apartment there, and I'm sure she'll let us stay with her. No cost. Only a jaunt to the food store – which we'd have to do anyway if we were down here."

I couldn't fight the logic. In a month we were in Philadelphia. Joseph Mallord William Turner was a pivotal figure in nine-teenth-century British painting. His canvases depicted nature on a massive scale and often in violent conflict with humans and their inventions. I was very moved by the exhibit. We spent nearly four hours moving through the galleries and another two nursing a couple of cappuccinos at a nearby café. It was a beau-tiful day in May. One of the happiest of my life.

Aisling brought out the best in me, and for that I was grate-ful. I really enjoyed who I was when I was with her. I liked her friend, Grace, as well. She lived near the university, in a spacious two-bedroom apartment (one bedroom of which was a well-stocked library).

"You can tell a lot about a person," I told Grace, "by the books she buys."

"Yes," Aisling added, "and by the way she organizes them."

Grace was about ten years older than Aisling. She had been working on a dissertation on the poetry of Thomas Hardy. "The trouble with Hardy . . ." she told us – she would begin each of the two or three conversations we had about her work with this phrase – "The trouble with Hardy was that he wrote each pub-lished poem with a different stanza structure. This makes it very difficult to understand his relationship to his medium. If I were working on Shakespeare's sonnets, for example, it would all be so much easier, because he repeated his form so often that it no longer became an issue."

"How close are you to finishing?" Aisling asked. "I remember the last time –"

Ah, the last time. I was closer then. It's so very difficult. I can't explain it to you."

"Can't you just finish it up even if it isn't perfect?" I asked.

Both women looked at me as if I were an apostate.

"What I mean is that sometimes you can't will a peak perfor-mance. I remember when I used to run track. I prepared the same way, week in and week out. However, when it came to the races, every so often I'd really pop a good time. It was almost as if it were outside my power. It just happened."

This was met with two blank stares.

"What I'm saying is that maybe competence is in our control but greatness is a gift of the gods. We can't control it or make it happen. I don't know. I'm not intending to be critical or anything."

It didn't sink in with Grace, but Aisling and I discussed the topic further on the way home.

"What I'm saying is that 'perfection' is impossible. It's a fiction in someone's mind. You can't be perfect. You shouldn't even try to be perfect." Aisling began gripping the steering wheel tightly with both hands. "It's not productive," I continued. "No one can be perfect. The Turkish rug makers used to have a tradition of putting a flaw in each of their rugs."

"Why?" Aisling asked.

"To show to God that they didn't aspire to perfection. The very thought would have been an instance of pride. And we all know that pride is the root of all evil."

"I thought that was money," Aisling said as she loosened her grip on the wheel and began steering with one hand again.

"I don't think Grace liked me," I said when we'd passed the Chesapeake House on the freeway back to Washington.

"Not at all," Aisling said. "She admires many of the same things I do about you. It's just that you can be a strange person to talk to at times, Michael."

"Strange?"

"Yes, you use such a moral tone at times."

"Really?"

"Yes. It's what made me stalk you when I first came to Fairview."

"You stalked me?"

"Yes. I was attracted to you but I didn't want to move too quickly. So I watched you from the shadows, a cautious predator sizing up her prey."

"I hope you don't intend to chew my head off."

"Well, I'm not a praying mantis, but Grace did say that I ought to marry you."

"She did? I'm beginning to like your friend Grace more and more."

It was really hard now for me to imagine living any other way. I mean, I had always wanted to go to Europe, but I had always imagined the trip differently. I had assumed that I would be moving between pensiones and riding in second-class train cars, using a Eurail pass. But with my newfound prosperity and the crowd that I'd run into in Paris, I found that life in four- and five-star hotels was much more comfortable.

I felt a little queer about resigning my teaching position at the last minute after the school year had finished. But I told myself that I'd been "riffed" too many times by the school district (that is, let go in June only to be rehired in August), that I didn't have too much sympathy for them. Besides, there were always plenty of new teachers aching to get into the Montgomery County public school system.

I was glad to be rid of the place.

But I did feel a bit guilty. Perhaps it was the boys on the cross-country team who I would be missing. After all, I had run the program for seven years. Now someone else would be getting up in the early morning to watch them puffing off into the fog.

The situation I was in was this: Mookie had gotten us rooms at the Ritz for a couple of nights and then the use of a rather large apartment on the Avenue Mozart. It was there that I met Terri. She was a young American woman of means whose daddy had made a killing in real estate before the market went bad. "Timing is everything, darling!"

Terri's timing was perfect for me. And she never worried about anything. She lived with Marc, who was a photographer – not for a living, you understand. Marc was set. But Marc liked to have something to do. So he took pictures. He developed pictures. He printed pictures, and he framed pictures.

Marc's place was decorated entirely with pictures he'd taken at various times. In his bedroom was a semi-revealing picture of Terri. He liked to show it to everyone who came by. It was one of his prize possessions. "What a sweet little ass she's got," Marc would say as he lifted his bushy black eyebrows.

"I know," I replied when he showed it to me.

"Let's get her to take off her clothes right now!"

"I have to be inspired," she responded.

"You have two admiring men here," Marc said.

"Not enough."

"Do you want three?"

"Darling, I can have all the men I want. Don't flatter yourselves."

And that would be that.

Things were going evenly I suppose. Along with the sculptor, Eogue (rhymes with fugue) and his companion, Angus, we formed a neat little group. Angus was the only one without any money. He was obviously taking Eogue for bucks. Angus was Scottish. Eogue was French, but he looked Slavic. During the day, Eogue would work on carving fireplace mantels. He had a set of mythological creatures that he would place in a tangle of vines. The creatures merely rearranged themselves from mantel to mantel. The vines remained the same.

The people who bought Eogue's mantels were mostly young people who knew him. They would go to his studio and see five or six freestanding mantels and exclaim over them. Eogue would enter into a discussion with them about art. When he talked, he moved his stubby fingers in the air. It was almost as if he were signing his speech at the same time, so precise were his gestures.

After a lecture on art, the acquaintance would have to have one of the mantels. Eogue always left a part of the mantel unfinished, so he could personalize it for the new owner. When a sale was complete, Eogue would have us over for a drink. Eogue liked to drink.

He would bring out an expensive wine for us all to admire while he drank cognac, VSOP. "It's an acquired taste, you know."

Mookie was not a part of this group. He was an entrepreneur. While I was living off the fat of the land, Mookie was moving up in the world. I suppose I was his good luck piece. For my part, Mookie kept me in spending money for just about anything I wanted.

Things were going well until our Oktoberfest trip to Munich. Marc, Terri, and I often took trips together. We'd rent separate rooms, and Terri would act according to her fancy. It wasn't too bad, really, because it relieved both Marc and me of having the entire responsibility of Terri at one time. She was more than any man could handle alone.

The Oktoberfest trip was different. Eogue and Angus were coming along. Then Angus scratched at the last minute, after a spat with Eogue. Well, Eogue wasn't going to let his "redhead" push him around – after all, it was *his* bankroll they lived on – so he told Angus to take a hike. And that was the end of that. Or so we thought.

We flew into Munich and stayed in a house of a friend of Eogue's (another artist with inherited cash). The house was within walking distance of the Oktoberfest fairgrounds so that we could partake in the revelry without much travel required.

I must say that my overall impression of Munich was more favorable than I had anticipated. The people were friendly and not stuffy, as I had always imagined Germans to be. Though I spoke no German, everyone seemed to know either French or English, so I was able to converse with virtually everybody. All I had to learn was the money.

On the way to the Oktoberfest grounds on the first day, a man offered Terri a white flower to put into her hair. She gratefully accepted and wore it the entire day. The music, the people, the general good-natured bustle put us all in a good mood.

It wasn't until the night of the third day, when we arrived home at around one in the morning, that we perceived something amiss. The door to the house was unlocked.

"I was sure I locked the damn thing," Eogue said. We believed this. Eogue was a stickler for details. The little giant of a man was particularly meticulous about them. (After all, details were what made his mantel vines so enchanting.)

Nobody said anything. I remember feeling very apprehensive. I twisted the tie cords of my red-hooded sweatshirt around my left index finger. We walked into the house and turned on the lights. In the sitting room in a chair was Angus. He had an almost empty bottle in his hand and his skin was almost as red as his fiery hair.

"A bit late, aren't we?" he said.

"Get out of here," Eogue demanded.

"That's not a good way to talk to a friend." Angus's speech was slurred.

"I told you it was over between us. Now get the hell out of here before I call the police."

Angus only laughed.

Eogue was furious and rushed at Angus. Halfway there, the tall slender Scot jumped up and lifted a hidden ax. But an ax didn't stop the little giant. He continued at his pace. Nothing was going to stop him from his aim – until Angus's aim got the better of him and laid him out. Down and out in one blow: a smash to the side of the head with the side of the head. The axhead, that is. Angus drew on the lore of his Scottish forefathers as he smote Eogue just above the ear with the flat of the axhead. The result was devastating. The mantel man, the stonemason, dropped hard upon the wooden floor, as cold as one of his stone mantels.

Then Angus turned toward us.

Chapter Eleven

"You're all in on this," slobbered the red-faced Scot.

We looked at this asshole in front of us brandishing a long-handled ax. We looked at Eogue lying at our feet with a trickling of blood from his temple where he'd been struck. And then we came to our conclusion together: run!

And run we did, as Angus pursued us to the door, but not out into the street. Marc, Terri, and I ran two blocks to the nearest major *strasse*. Luckily there was a taxi coming on the opposite side of the street. Marc ran to it, flagging it down, as I held a shivering Terri in my arms. The taxi driver spoke rapid German, which Marc understood but I did not.

Marc motioned us over.

"He's only got room for two," Marc began in a different tone of voice than I had ever heard him use. It was dead, cold, stonelike. It reminded me of Eogue lying on the floor. Seriously hurt. Possibly dead.

"Come on, Terri," he said in French.

I was the one holding her with my arm. But she went to him. Never a hesitation. Just like that. And it was over. Not even a "sorry, old man."

I was left alone.

Thoughts and feelings were racing through my consciousness so that I didn't know who I was entirely or what I was doing. I felt disoriented, betrayed, and empty. I pulled the red hood of my sweatshirt over my head and started toward a bench to sit down. There was a little bit of urban park there surrounded by a four-foot dark metal fence. Just then I heard the sound of European police sirens: whooo haaa, whooo haaa, whooo haaa. They were coming from my right. As I turned to confirm what I heard, I was arrested by the sounds from my left of shoes hitting the pavement. I turned to see another man wearing a red hooded sweatshirt running hard in my direction.

It wasn't difficult to apprehend that I was at the wrong place at the wrong time. My previous frenzy now reached a new level. The fugitive gave me a fleeting glance without breaking stride. I thought he seemed to smile, but the lighting wasn't very good. The man ran to the very same bench where I had been heading and in one fluid motion planted his left foot on the cement, jumping to the bench, and then with his right foot on the flat seat sprang forward – over the fence with inches to spare. In a moment he was gone.

Seconds later I was feeling the grasp of police putting humane plastic handcuffs on my wrists and dragging me toward the patrol car. They were barking at me, but I didn't understand a word of it. I was totally defeated.

In the car, my body was involuntarily shaking. It wasn't really cold, but I was shaking. There was nothing I could do about it. I opened my eyelids as far as I could. My eyes began to roll around in my head. I didn't like the feeling. I hadn't had that much to drink, but I was overcome with the vision of Eogue lying there on that floor. Bleeding. Dying. My running. Marc and Terri deserting me. I saw that taxi. There had been room for three. Marc was just bullshitting me. And like a sucker, I had taken it. I took his bullshit. Then I vomited.

I sat in a jail cell. There were four of us. It did not take a speaking knowledge of German to understand what was before me in the jail cell: Old Age, Sickness, and Death. These were my companions in the cell.

Old Age. One man long in years but short in happiness was drunk out of his skull. He was reciting poetry and singing popular songs. No one paid any attention to him until he tried for a high note. It wavered slightly before it cracked and then precipitously fell to the ground shattered. Not to be daunted, he tried again and again. It was at these moments that the old fart risked being hit with a shoe by the runt who was sitting next to me. The younger man was doing badly and had taken off his shoes, which he intended to use as weapons – or the threat of weapons.

The shoes. The vaudeville-era hook. How indignant a response from an audience who cannot appreciate true worth! (Ah! But what is true worth? It is the standard of taste that exists in any respectable jail cell. Respectable jail cell? *Sans doute!* The audience is the criminal, not the poet. *Mais non*, the poet is always a criminal. You must remember *Ich spreche nicht Deutsch*. What I do speak is the language of loneliness and betrayal.)

How sad the fate of the old. The old considers the allotment of years. Seventy-two are given to most of us in this era. Anything over that is a gift of the gods. So how is it that I mark my age? Do I understand my own aging? He did not remember getting this old.

Are all men or only this one subject to age? The broken-yellow-toothed gray-haired man leaned on one of the bunks because his body was crooked and bent.

This old singer had family. In between musical numbers, he showed me (since no one else was interested) some snapshots of the grandkids – or at least of some kids. This was how we communicated. Pictures show no partiality to language. I wondered if these kids actually knew the old man. I wonder if they knew what he was going through. Preparing to die. Alone. Afraid. So what of that?

So what of that? There's not much you can do about it. But there is despair. Despair. It can be positive or negative. In a positive way, it can send you to a new appreciation of who you are and where you are going in life. In a negative way, it can make you long for the finality of death. Not that you want it, but that if it is presented to you, the struggle against the anxiety can become too much. Better just to end it. You can never match up. Never. What are the desires of the young person? To be famous, have lots of women (or men), and to have riches. These are sought as ends in and of themselves. Ends in themselves. But they are not ends in themselves.

No, they are means to another end: tranquility. We want to be transported to tranquility, satisfied with *who* we are and *what* we are. *That* we are is a given. We had nothing to do with it. How unfair. To be presented with such a problem. A problem for which I had no language to communicate. Remember, I spoke no German.

Old age. So much gone. Opportunities lost. Justice served. Who wants justice? The very thought of it makes me shiver again.

Sickness. The man-child with the shoes. Short, with delicate features. When he began to scratch his skin, I saw the track marks on his arm. Mainliner. Crashing. Soon he might go crazy. The shoes were only the first sign. He was readying himself for battle. It would be a battle that he regularly fought – whenever he couldn't get a fix. So young. In so much pain.

Why must there be drug addicts? What possesses someone to hurt himself in such a way? But then, he doesn't believe he's hurting himself, making himself sick. He knows that the needle will get him high. And he knows that the needle is making him very sick. It is ruining his body. Both things are understood at the same time. But the addict does not take the needle for the sake of ruining the body. No. He does it to get high. And though he knows the other proposition at the same time, it is as if it were hidden by a veil. He doesn't have to look at it. All that he clearly sees is a means to get high. His attention is diverted from what is partially hidden by the veil.

Is his sickness his own fault? Yes. But now it is beyond his control. So many things are beyond our control. Not everything, but too many.

Sometimes blame gets all jumbled up. I can hear the clear voice of justice. It is my father's voice. But was it justice when the plane crash took his life? Or was it justice that so much money should fall to me? Or justice that the red-hooded sweatshirt they put into jail was me? Had I become sick, too?

The third man wore fine clothes, but they seemed baggy on him. He was gaunt and fading away. I wondered whether he was dying of AIDS. So young. So young to be at Death's door. He seemed resigned. I wondered what his crime was.

A sweep of gay bars? Black-market promises for a cure? The young man looked sadly out of place. Youth and death are unnatural pairs, just as his well-made suit was not appropriate prison garb. Who was going to comfort him in the end? Or would he die as many others, alone, frantic, choking on his own vomit?

Death. He did not sit in the cell, yet he was a companion to us all. His name is emptiness, but he is so frightening that we cannot bear to look at him. None of us did. A little secret of sorts: You see, if you are not prepared to meet your date, you will feel awkward. How absurd to find that your date does not like the corsage that you have purchased. So uncouth. Perhaps it is an obliteration of consciousness. Socrates described this option, death, as a sleep without dreams. Who doesn't aspire to a sleep without dreams – unless, that is, you don't wake up at the end. The unknown. The empty.

Is it rational to fear that which is unknown? You are put into either Heaven or Hell, or you are reborn or you are extinguished on the hearth of the fire of being. Hell is a pretty bad alternative. No doubt about it. I would not choose it under any circumstance. That's why I don't believe in Hell. But in all true humility, my belief doesn't matter at all. Not at all.

Then why should I even think about it? Because I must. Because we all must. Death is that appointment we try to keep putting off. It is not something we like to consider in youth and innocence. But our subjective disposition matters naught. It is an appointment we will have to keep.

Aside from Hell, what could be so bad? Well, to be born into a lower form of life, or into a situation that tries the soul. Isn't that what life is all about: trying the soul?

I did not like to think that way. I had never been very good at tests of character. I didn't score very high.

Bummer.

Even the better alternatives, such as dissolving into nothingness or going to Heaven to be at one with God (again, dissolving into a nothingness that *is*) didn't sound so great to me.

What I really wanted was to be able to continue as I had been. To be a young man. To have my father alive again.

A Story of Aisling – Part Five

It was during the second year of her doctoral program at the University of Pennsylvania that Aisling's favorite professor, Jerry Tatum, asked her to stop by his office. Professor Tatum (he encouraged everybody to call him Jerry) always kept a sign-up sheet on his door so that students could prearrange appointments and not have to wait around forever (as was the case with many other professors). Aisling went to the office door to sign up and found that her name was already written in for the last appointment of the day. It was a little inconvenient, but she would manage it by calling her supervisor at the library and having him shift her hours slightly. (Most students who worked at the library did not go in for such niceties, but Aisling didn't want to get paid for work she hadn't done.)

When she stopped by Professor Tatum's office, the door was ajar. She approached and listened carefully to determine whether there was another student inside. She was ten minutes early. She heard no one.

Gingerly, she rapped on the thick, solid mahogany door. She hardly made a sound, but her knock was instantly greeted. "Is that you, Aisling?"

Aisling came in and sat down. Professor Tatum had a spacious corner office with a great view. To the left was a smallish desk with a computer on it. (Professor Tatum had been one of the first English teachers at Penn to turn to the computer for his scholarly writing.) Along two walls were floor-to-ceiling bookcases crammed full of books, many of them double shelved. On the other side of the room was a long sofa. Jerry waved to Aisling to sit on the sofa. So she did. In a moment he had shut the door and was sitting next to her.

"I wanted to talk to you about the paper you turned in on Milton."

Aisling tightened up. Her knees were pressed closely together. Jerry held her paper in one hand and stretched the other out against the back of the couch. He was thirtyish and wore a beard.

"This use of contemporary political events to explain 'Samson Agonistes' is very interesting. Of course, during the Nixon years there were pop attempts at this, but this is sterling."

Aisling tried to smile. She pulled down at her skirt despite the fact that it wasn't hiked up even a centimeter.

"This was easily the best essay in the class. In fact, I think it's good enough for publication – with some revisions, of course."

What was he saying? Aisling's mind was confused.

"For example, you need to establish more completely the intellectual context by which your use of domestic politics and the associated events can enlighten and make more relevant the plot of the poem. To do this you need to make reference to some body of critical literary theory."

"Thank you," Aisling replied. She didn't know what else to say.

"I would suggest Aristotle's *Poetics* – particularly the sections on the relationship between 'thought' and 'spectacle' – along with some Foucault on bringing the medieval episteme into the modern world."

"Yes, of course."

"I'd be happy to look at a revision. I have a friend who is the editor at *Milton Studies* who I'm sure would love this. I'd be happy to set things up for you. After all, if you're going to make a career of this, you've got to get some publications under your belt – even before you get your doctorate." Professor Jerry inched closer and set the essay in Aisling's lap. She stared at the paper, not looking up. Then, Professor Jerry stroked her leg above the knee. Her dress began to hike up. He repeated his caressing, this time on her bare leg going toward her underwear. Aisling stood up abruptly.

"Thank you. I'll get right to it. Very kind of you."

Professor Jerry touched her arm lightly. "It really is very good, Aisling. Something to be proud of."

"You're very kind," she said standing up and making for the door. "I'll get right to it. Thank you for taking an interest in me." Aisling delivered her words to her shoes, which needed polishing.

Professor Jerry laughed. "Not at all, Aisling. Just stop by when you make those changes. It's really a good essay. With a little *private coaching* it could be professional quality."

Aisling went to the library and did her job. Then she went back to her apartment. She stuck the essay in a drawer, where it stayed until May, when she withdrew from the doctoral program.

And so I sat among these three whose names I would never know: Old Age, Sickness, and Death. In a foreign prison at night. The events of the preceding day had been too much for me. I longed for sleep but it never seemed to come.

So much care. So much worry: *With careful diligence even the dust on the windowpane shall be wiped away.*

Or was it like this? So much care. So much worry: *The dust and the window, together, shall fade away.* All within. All without. It doesn't matter. My life depends upon it.

The next morning I was released. A man who spoke English said there had been some mistake. They had thought that I was someone else who had been mixed up in a barroom brawl. But they had gotten the culprit, and so now I was free.

It was strange, but I didn't feel free.

What had been so difficult before (such as finding the train station), was now a simple task. I bought my ticket and took a seat to wait for my train. I looked squarely at the large electronic black sign with white moveable letters that fanned down like a thousand playing cards that shuffled just the right information on the trains arriving and departing. I became immersed in the constant movement of the cards constantly being shuffled by their computer croupiers as they recorded the comings and goings. What a constant change was. And yet within those changes there were structures: the train schedule. A promise to perform – but for conditions beyond control. Whose control?

I arose from my seat and headed *not* for my train platform, but back to the house I'd abandoned the night before. I couldn't depart Munich until I'd gone back to Eogue.

When I got to the house I noticed several things: One, there were no police; two, there were no signs that police had been there; three, a light was on inside and I could hear music. I had returned prepared to be a witness. Prepared to face Angus.

And face Angus I did. It was he who answered the door. "Ah, Michael, come in. We're just making breakfast. Eogue's doing the tea." It was noon, but that didn't matter.

I allowed myself to be led inside. We walked through the room where the struggle had taken place. I never considered that Angus's invitation might be a ruse for him to take care of a witness to his crime. The thought never formed in my mind, but what did appear was the solid form of Eogue in the kitchen in an apron, making toast and tea.

"I've tried teaching Eogue how to make a real Scottish breakfast with bacon, sausage, and eggs, but it's hard to penetrate that marble skull of his." Angus smiled when he said this. I suddenly realized that his arm was around my shoulder.

"Mon ami," Eogue said. "You look like you've seen a spirit." He wore a plaster on the side of his face.

"Are you all right, Eogue?"

"What *this?*" Eogue made a sweeping gesture with his hand and chuckled.

"A lovers' spat," returned Angus as he seated me at the table and handed me a piece of toast.

The schedule board of the train station looked different now. There seemed to be less cosmic significance to it than there had been only six hours before, when I had been sitting in the same seat. Did the fact that we had been wrong about the fate of Eogue make any difference in the way Marc and Terri had treated me? They didn't know that ax play was just a little roughhouse among lovers. Eogue had been lying on the floor, senseless, bleeding. This was a fact. We three had taken him for dead. This was a fact.

The three of us had run because we were afraid. Afraid of being hacked to bits by Angus. Afraid of being questioned by the police. Afraid of standing up to Angus on behalf of our friend Eogue. This was also, sadly, a fact.

Thus, when we hit the street, we were in a Hobbesian state of nature. Every man for himself. They paired up. They headed out. But why did they exclude me? There was only one explanation: part of their self-preservation plan was setting me up to get caught. They would escape, and the police would get somebody. Somebody who spoke no German. It was the only interpretation I could make.

One has time to think on a train ride. I decided that what had happened was simply that Marc and Terri decided to chuck it all: Eogue, Angus, and me. They took off for another life. I was left alone with chance events: a barroom brawler with a red sweatshirt just like mine. There was no purpose to any of it. I spent a night in jail for nothing.

By the time I reached Paris, I was certain that I needed a change from the life I had been living. I was the black-and-white train board with the cards constantly shuffling away – except that the changes in me were occurring without a schedule. They were random. Accidental. Driven only by my desire to satiate myself. I was seeking something. But what was it?

I recalled a time when I took a subway ride in Chicago, getting off at Hyde Park, at the Garfield and Fifty-fifth Street stop. Not twenty feet from the steps were a couple of old guys drinking pint bottles of booze out of paper bags. They were sitting there on the stoop side by side, drinking and staring up at a billboard of two young, successful African Americans with all the trinkets that constituted the good life in the US of A. The trinkets that signified that one had arrived. But these two men would never arrive. They were sitting there at eleven in the morning getting drunk and staying drunk. Getting nowhere. And staying there.

Still, they sat there dreaming of what would never be. Dreaming and drinking. Hooked by advertisers just as much as they were hooked by hooch.

And then I remembered the needle tracks on the arm of the boy in the German jail cell. What was it that drove his life? Was it the same thing that had been driving mine?

I had two stops I wanted to make in Paris. First, I wanted to go to our apartment and write a note to Mookie, to ask him for more money. Second, I wanted to go to the American Express office for our mail. (Mookie didn't think it was a good idea to receive mail at the apartment.)

When I got to the Avenue Mozart apartment, I was surprised to see Mookie there. I was also surprised to see him packing.

"What's up?" I asked as I walked in.

"Oh, yeah. I'm glad you're here, actually. You can help me load this trunk." Some things never change. I got down onto the floor where he had everything in a heap.

"You take what's yours and put it in that suitcase over there," he said.

"Why are you packing?"

"Got to go."

"Why do you have to go?"

"Some things didn't work out. Say, are you going to talk or work?"

"Is there a deadline or something?"

"Yeah. *Dead*line is a good way to put it."

I didn't know how to understand Mookie. I knew the crowd he hung around with, so I decided to keep my mouth shut and question him when we had gotten out of there.

We were in a taxi driving to Charles de Gaulle Airport. Mookie canvassed the area and finally decided everything was all right. He relaxed in his seat.

"So what's the situation?"

"Not here," he said.

"Then where?" Mookie's penchant for security seemed a bit ridiculous at times.

"Patience."

"Where am I going?"

"Trust."

"What if I don't want to go where you're going?"

Mookie smiled a knowing smile and put his hand on my shoulder. His gaunt features made him seem older than his years. "Chill, Michael. You're only going a few steps with me now. Where I'm headed you won't be able to follow. Even if you wanted to."

I decided to wait.

At the airport, we got out of the taxi and walked our baggage to a waiting area. Mookie told me to sit with the luggage because they had signs all around that unattended luggage would be confiscated (bomb threats and all that). Then he walked off.

Soon he returned and told me to check his bags on a flight to Rio under his name. "They'll ask to see my passport," I said.

Mookie gave me his passport. "What if they figure out that the picture on your passport does not match my face?"

"Then come back for me. Don't invent problems, compadre."

I did what he told me to do. They didn't look at the picture.

When I got back to the waiting area, Mookie took the plane ticket and then got up and started walking, holding my suitcase as if it were his. I followed him. We took the airport shuttle to the rental car section of the airport. Mookie rented a car in my name and we walked over to pick it up. (No free lift to your vehicle.)

He handed me the car keys. "Drive around," he said.

"What's this all about?" I asked.

"Leave the airport and then drive around. Practice coming in and leaving near the international gate."

We made two or three passes until Mookie was confident that I knew the lay of the land. Then we exited the airport grounds and drove around the vicinity.

"Things are upset a bit," he began. "My people, my allies, are mixing it up a bit, and for a player of my size it's time to clear out."

"The police?"

Mookie laughed. "I wish it were only the police. No. The police aren't even in the picture. But our arrangement is finished."

"What do you mean, 'finished'?"

"I put a final payment to you in the Crédit Lyonnais bank, under your name and this account number." He handed me a slip of paper. "There's fifty grand in that account. I'm sorry we couldn't keep going together, but if you knew the whole picture, you'd understand."

"What about the house back home?"

"Home?"

"You know, DC."

"Oh, if there's anything in that Potomac house you want, you better have someone put it in storage for you in the next week or two. The locks may be changed at any time."

"Great," I said.

"You have anything there that you'd die for?"

"No."

"I thought not. Just a bunch of stuff. I remember when I left Vietnam. No home. No parents. No nothing. Sometimes you have to move on."

There was no more time to talk. Mookie wanted to return to the airport and have me drop him off as we had practiced. I did it. As he was getting out of the rented car, I asked him when I had to return it.

"Whenever you want, man. I've already paid for twenty-four hours."

That was the last I ever saw of Mookie.

I drove around awhile, cruising over the area I'd just passed with Mookie. I thought about Mookie and how little I knew about him. How untrustworthy he would seem to most people compared with "respectable" people like Sara and Bernie, for example, and yet how he was the only one who had not let me down. He had kept his promises.

I didn't know just how much money Mookie had given me in the seven months or so since we became "partners." It wasn't a lot I suppose, compared with the size of the original stake. But it had all gone toward changing my way of life.

With Bernie, the swindle had been calculated and surgical. But with Mookie, I'd gotten exactly what he'd promised. And while it lasted, it was good. Besides, there was fifty thousand sitting in a bank for me. With judicious use, I could live awhile on that until my rolling certificate of deposit started maturing.

I turned the rental car in and took a bus back to the city center, this time to the Left Bank. Back to the quarter near the Cluny Museum, where accommodations could be had more cheaply.

I decided to go over to the post office to phone about the boxing up of a few of my things back in DC. The only person I could think of to do this was Angie Santini.

In some respects, I felt bad about Angie. We had seen a lot of each other before I left for Paris, but then again, I had never promised her anything. Her dad, Vic, had pressed hard for me to become his son-in-law (especially when he found out about the money I had fallen into). But there never had been any promises. Never.

I remember that when I told Angie that I was taking an extended trip to Europe, she had asked if she should "wait for me." I told her to do what she liked. I didn't know if I were ever coming home.

So I felt a bit uncomfortable calling her now.

International calls are such a bother. There's the time difference and the hassle of international operators and the awkward payment arrangement at the post office. After all this, the party very likely would not be home. But today I was in luck, because the phone was picked up on the second ring. However, the voice was not Angie's.

"Yeah, I'll get her." I knew that voice, but I couldn't place it. "Michael? Is that you?" Angie came on the line.

"I didn't mean to interrupt you," I began. "I've just got a favor to ask you."

"Where are you, Michael?"

"France. Paris."

"How do you like Paris?"

"Oh, pretty well, I guess. I'll be over here some time, I think. So I was going to ask you – "

"Things have been fine here, too. Did you hear Bob Crouter and I are going to be married in two weeks?"

Bob Crouter. That was who had picked up the phone. Of course, Computer Bob. Angie had been going with him when I started seeing her. Perhaps my influence had gotten him off the mark.

"That's great. Congratulations."

"Bob's business has taken off. He quit Fairview the same time you did. It caused quite a scramble, I can tell you."

"Yes. I can imagine."

"It's all so exciting. We're going to buy a big house at the end of the school year. I think I'll quit, too. No sense in working if you don't need the money."

"Sounds sensible, Angie. Say, about this favor – "

The phone started beeping. It was her call-waiting feature. "Look, I've got another call on the line. I'll talk with you later."

"Right, Angie. Congratulations again."

I guess I got what I deserved. I no longer served any purpose for Angie. We had gone our separate ways. I despaired for a time as I sat in my tiny attic hotel room. I had gotten a special price on the room because you couldn't stand up in half of it. The bed was positioned next to the lowest part of the slanting roof so that if I lay on the edge of the bed there was perhaps six inches between my nose and the aging plaster ceiling.

I stayed in Paris two weeks. It gave me time to think. Through the US embassy I found a company that would box and store my things back in DC (though they were expensive). In one way it was a silly gesture. I had been living fine without those things. What made me think I needed them now?

I found that my ideas about many things were beginning to change. For starters, I decided to move to London.

Chapter Twelve

A Story of Aisling – Part Six

It was late August. I had been dating Aisling since Christmas. I was beginning to get a glimpse of who she was and why I was so attracted to her. First, she was unlike any other woman I had ever met in my life. She wanted nothing from me. I could be with her and simply interact with her. She seemed inclined to accept me as I was and to highlight those aspects of my character that she most appreciated. Thus, by contrast, when I failed in the execution of my intention (a frequent flaw of mine), she merely held up to me the image of me at my best. It was up to me to make the connection.

One of the most enjoyable activities in Washington during August is to row on the C&O (Chesapeake and Ohio) Canal. The canal begins in Georgetown and ends somewhere north – White's Ferry, I think. The canal was begun in the early nineteenth century as a way of promoting commerce. It was constructed with a number of locks and a towpath on which draft animals would tow the vessels toward the destination. Today you can simulate the trip by going to Great Falls National Park, in Maryland. Here, people in historical costume will put you on a replica barge and move you back and forth between locks.

Digging the C&O Canal was an enormous project. Their construction used cutting-edge technology, but unfortunately took too long to complete. Before it was done, the Baltimore and Ohio Railroad had stolen its market. Not only could the railroads convey the same amount of goods that the barges could, but they could do it in a fraction of the time.

How sad – obsolete before it was even finished.

Somehow, the canal resonates with me as a personal metaphor. Obsolete before it is complete. To be obsolete is to be of no value. Like most Americans, this bothers me. I wanted to stand for something. Did this mean that I wanted Andy Warhol's fifteen minutes of fame? Perhaps. Did I really aspire to have my picture on the cover of *People* magazine? Oh, *please*. But why not?

Aisling and I procured a rowboat at Swain's boathouse and began rowing on the C&O Canal. Unlike the walkers, joggers, and cyclists on the towpath, we were actually reenacting some of the process that was vaguely connected to the canal's original purpose.

As you move through the brackish water with fifty other boats, there is a sense that you are traveling at a slower pace. It is a way of transporting your spirit back into history, to an age when important decisions were made at a pace that more approximated our ability to reason.

As we moved forward, we passed a large continuous hill of green on our right, which seemed rustic and wild. On our left was the towpath filled with people. Beyond the towpath was the Potomac River: an old symbol of our nation's democracy.

"Do you like to row?" Aisling asked after we had been on the water for about fifteen minutes.

"Ah, this is easy rowing. Next time, we'll rent a canoe and glide through the water like a bug."

"Just what I've always aspired to be." She laughed.

"Oh well, we have to live with reality sometimes."

"Speak for yourself," she said.

"Ha! You're one to talk. You left your PhD program to teach at Fairview."

"You know why I left."

"No, I don't. Look Aisling, Fairview may be all right for the likes of me, but you're destined for far more. I love you too much not to say so. You deserve to be somewhere that can really let you grow and become the person I already know you want to be."

Aisling looked blankly at me. Then she turned her head and pointed to a family of three riding a bicycle-built-for-three on the towpath. "I've never seen that before," she said. "If they fall off, they'll all get wet."

"And if they worried too much about getting wet, then they'd never get anywhere," I replied.

Again silence.

The ride was ended by the lock, which marked the "turn-around" point. We had already reached it. Now it was time to come home.

During the week, I thought over what Aisling and I had talked about. I wouldn't let it rest. I called a friend of mine who used to teach at Fairview and was now taking a master's degree in political science at Georgetown.

"So, why do you want to get a PhD in English?" Joel asked playfully.

"I don't," I replied.

"So what's the issue?"

"I just wanted to know if you knew of any programs overseas or anything. You see I have a friend . . ."

"Yeah. Right. A friend."

"Don't shit me, Joel. This friend is really not set up to enter a program in the US. Too many side issues. I think she has to clear out and go somewhere else."

"Okay. Say you're correct. And say your friend isn't *you* but really someone else. Let's just say that. Well, then there's the issue of language. Unless your 'friend' is fluent in another language, he'll have to study in Britain, Canada, Australia, or New Zealand."

"Britain would be best."

"Well, there's a foreign studies office in Georgetown, at the new Healey Center. Try there. All they can do is throw you out."

"It's not for *me*."

"Right."

"I'm serious."

"Say hello to your friend for me."

And that's how I got started. I went to the center and looked over the literature. They had application forms and everything. I took out material for Oxford, Cambridge, the University of London, Manchester, and Durham.

You have to understand, it wasn't that I wanted Aisling to leave my life; it was just that I loved her too much to want her to stay at Fairview.

We worked on her applications together. And when she was admitted (with a grant for women scholars from a US foundation), we celebrated: coffee and dessert at Papa Giovanni's. Were we engaged? I don't know. We made no formal pledge. I thought in my heart of hearts that she was probably gone from me forever.

Why would I do it? Why would I send away the person I loved more than anyone? I guess you could say that was the reason. I loved her too much.

Aisling had stopped writing about the time I moved into the big house in Potomac. I don't really blame her. It had been about six months since I had written her. Still, she had continued writing on her own for a time. And in a strange way I somehow expected her to continue to do so.

In fact, when I picked up my mail at the American Express office in Paris after returning from Germany, I half expected to see one of Aisling's letters forwarded to me.

There was only one letter waiting for me in Paris. It contained just a little card. A funeral memorial with a Bible verse on the back. Father Mac had died.

I don't know why I was surprised. Father Mac was overweight and he smoked and drank too much. But there had been something about that man that had always seemed immortal to me. He had found a peace that I never had. I guess that made him one of the most successful men I had ever known.

Death. Once again. The prison cell. How long might it be until I would be free?

It was a rough crossing. In late November the waters in the Channel can get choppy. It had been just over a year since the advent of my Great Expectations. Was I any better off? I had been drinking a bitter lemon at the bar when I decided that I needed some air. Everyone was getting sick because of the motion of the boat. I knew that I'd have to go back in to get my suitcase on Deck 1 that was on the third level of the stainless steel racks, but just now I did not want to join the retching masses.

Outside there was a steady spray of light rain and gusty wind. It was evening and the boat appeared headed for Hell. I did not know how or why I was traveling to England or what I expected to find there. What would be there that wasn't in France?

What was I going to do when my money ran out?

My ticket took me to Victoria Station. It was eleven o'clock at night and I thought I should get some accommodation. I tried calling one of those "hotel room finders" from the train station, but they had all closed at ten. I had a choice: staying up all night or checking into a fleabag.

I was too tired to stay up all night. Besides, it was raining. Within three blocks from the train station, I found a place with muslin sheets that didn't smell too bad, so I took that. Quite a come-down from four- and five-star hotels. But somehow that phase of my life now seemed to be a blip. I was back to a lifestyle with which I was more familiar.

"When a man is tired of London, a man is tired of life." Somebody once said that. Perhaps it was Aisling. But I did not come to England to hang out in London. I had a journey to make, and the sooner I started, the better it would be. I took out some paper and began to plan. It was hopeless. I didn't know what I wanted to do. Instead I wrote a letter to Aisling. She was one of the few people who might understand what I was going through at the moment. And I desperately wanted someone to understand it all. Because I certainly didn't.

November 21, 1991

Dear Aisling,

It's been a while since I've written to you. About a year, to be exact. I'm sorry for the delay, but some strange things have been happening to me. Things that I'm not quite able to sort out. It's a very long story, but my life has been tumbled all about.

First, I quit my job teaching at Fairview. I am presently unemployed.

Second, I had been going around with my former neighbor, Mookie. I don't know if you ever met him. He's the most honest crook I've ever met. That sounds bad, I know, but you have to understand that the entire premise of my life has been altered. From nowhere to – I don't know what. (That's what John Locke used to call real essences.)

Third, Sara got married. (She's finally out of my life.)

Fourth, I have no permanent address. I will receive mail for a time at the American Express office at the Haymarket (though I am not in London, except in this most technical way).

Fifth, Father Mac died.

Sixth, I met these three guys in a German jail who deeply disturbed me (though, as you may remember, I speak no German).

Seventh, there was another guy who almost killed someone with an ax.

This must sound like the outpourings of a severely disturbed mind. Perhaps it is. What I do know is that I must make a journey.

Where I'm going, I don't know. I write these things to you because of all the people I've known, you seem to see things about me that I can't, and because writing something down makes it all seem official.

I wish I had been a better correspondent.

Michael

I bought the stamp, mailed the letter, and then went to a bookstore for a guidebook. I didn't know what I was looking for exactly. There were so many travel books. I wanted to know something about where I was going, wherever that might be, but I wasn't looking for Baedeker's or a Michelin guide.

The used-book section was always more to my taste. I love the musty smell of old books, a universal odor that transcends national boundaries. I spent all afternoon. I settled for Blakely's *Tour of the British Isles*. It was an old book published just after the Second World War. It wouldn't tell me where to stay or what to eat, but there was something about it that appealed to me. I hoped to be able to find my way.

Part Three

Chapter Thirteen

So much for the guidebook. The more I read, the more I realized that this was not really what I was looking for.

> No trip to the South is complete without visiting the fine country estates at Knole, Chartwell, and Penshurst. Here is afforded a style of life that is sadly declining in our post-War retrenchment of the once glorious Empire.

I didn't know what I was looking for, but since the Blakely book advised beginning in the south, I decided to go north. My first stop was Oxford. I don't know why I decided to go there, but I had always wanted to haunt Blackwell's Bookshop.

From the train station, I walked to the tourist accommodation center and found a bed-and-breakfast only a half-mile away. The place was located in an area called Jericho. It looked fine from the front, a two-story brick building that presented itself just like every other building on the block. The landlady, a Mrs Flighte, gave me a room on the first floor. It had no bath or toilet and looked out over a busy street. I lifted up the pillow and inspected it for cleanliness. The sheets seemed ok, though rather rough. The room itself was rather small – maybe six foot by ten foot. But how long would I stay in a room besides sleeping?

I gave Mrs Flighte a deposit and set out for a walk. I felt happy to see all the activity about me. The old city, with its stone architecture and its buildings that seemed to lean this way and that, were comforting to a man whose academic interests had always inclined toward history.

I didn't buy a map. I preferred just to wander about. When I got tired, I sat down. When I got hungry, I went into a food store or a pub for a bracer. It was on my second day there that I found Blackwell's. It wasn't as expansive as Foyle's nor as popularly oriented as Dillon's. No. It was in a class all its own. Dark wood paneling. Attentive and knowledgeable staff. Obscure titles that had to sit on the shelves for years before they were purchased. But just having them there gave the shop the feel of a fine library rather than a mercantile venture.

I decided to do some extensive browsing. The milieu of the place put me in a frame of mind that bordered on reverence. So many great minds were kept alive on the shelves. So many books were there that would never be displayed at the chain bookstores. Here was a repository of culture. The spines of the books quietly displayed what they were, but it took an aficionado to know what they really had to offer. I spent the whole day there and didn't buy a single book.

As I left, a young woman said to me, "I hope you were able to find what you wanted." But that was just the point. I didn't know what I wanted. Or whether "wanting" was the form of the question. The bookstore represented to me all the learning that I was lacking. I knew just enough to know that I could read a book a day for the rest of my life and still be woefully ignorant.

Why was it that in Bacon's day a learned man could have read everything there was? And now in our modern day, new books are being created at the rate of fifty thousand new volumes per year.

I left the bookstore and walked to a pub set off by itself, The Olde Boar, a white stuccoed building supported by visible, slanted timbers. The place was dark, with low lighting, black woodwork, and grime on the floor, and was teeming with people, mostly a university crowd. I slid my way to the bar and ordered a pint.

When I was on my second drink, a woman whom I took to be a few years younger than I, approached me and asked in a broad Northern English accent if I was "Kenny."

"Kenny? I could be," was my reply.

She laughed. Her short darkish hair bounced with the movement of her head (the light was too dim to determine the exact hue). She seemed animated. "Well, are you here for the lecture?"

"Isn't everybody?"

She smiled again. "Well, I'm here to get you to drink up. We're to be leaving straight away."

I saluted, and lifted my tankard.

The lecture was held over in a college hall whose name I didn't catch. I followed the mass of people from the pub and settled myself as close as possible to the woman who had piqued my interest.

The room was paneled in light oak. One wall had large rectangular windows that let in a considerable amount of the outside world. I imagined that in the daytime it would be a striking room.

The audience was 90 percent college age. Of that group about 70 percent were male. One older man who sat behind me kept muttering to the man next to him about how it was a disgrace that the students no longer attended lectures robed. I was rather amused by his tirade, but I didn't turn around to get a good look at him. I didn't want to let him know I was listening to him. The man seemed to think that lax attitudes toward lecture attire were partially responsible for the decline of the British Empire. I wondered if he'd ever read Blakely's *Tour of the British Isles*.

The students, seated in little groups, struck me as just like those in the United States. Some were chatting about social things, others about which authors they were reading; others were trying as hard as they could to be impressive about their learning. Finally, there were the lone wolves, who dressed oddly and had their noses in books (only occasionally coming up for air).

The robed speaker, an historian, spoke on "Side Changing in the English Civil War Period of 1642." The man talked in a halting fashion, making many digressions. He drank from a ceramic mug that was supposed to be coffee but which I suspected to be laced with whiskey.

The substance of the talk was why people in the time of the English civil strife that preceded the war were called upon to choose sides between Charles and Cromwell. You had to be "with us or against us." The problem was that so much of English society depended upon preferment that anyone who chose the wrong side could literally be ruined. Thus it was most conservative to take a position that could be modified if future circumstances altered. Perhaps you could be a Royalist with Cromwellian leanings or vice versa. A bolder approach would be to choose sides. If you picked the winner, you won big. You might get a fine job. But if you lost, you'd have to leave the country. Most people chose the conservative fence-sitting position. I guess things never change. Maybe it's the social pressure to conform, or maybe we just don't know our minds. But it seems to me that people love to congregate at a point that offers them the most options to move one way or the other. We look at figures such as Cromwell and think he's either a mad zealot or a saint with a mission.

"What makes a man like that thirst for power?" a pock-faced young man asked during the Q&A.

The speaker took a long sip from his mug and said, "I don't really think, actually, that Cromwell was a man thirsting for power, but rather for truth. He felt compelled to the position that was historically his. If he had turned his back upon it, then he'd have been abandoning truth. That's why many of his followers were so intolerant of the side switchers."

Michael Boylan

"Thirsting for power. Thirsting for truth. What's the difference?" the young man replied. "You still want what you don't have. Wasn't it Hobbes who said that overreaching for what you don't have was the primary sin of man?"

"I take it Hobbes was talking about the sin of pride. Some will always attack a leader and label him as being afflicted with too much pride."

The pock-faced youth sat down dissatisfied. Later in the pub (a different one for the post-talk discussion) the young man tried to address anyone who would listen to him. "This bloody bastard is talking the same kind of shit that all of them do. Pride my ass. Overreaching means taking more than your bloody share. We've all got to share and not be after more than comes our way!"

At first a number of people listened to the barroom orator, but then someone handed him a drink to shut him up, and he reconvened his court over at a corner table. The group I was in comprised the dark-haired Northern girl, who was called Gloria, her boyfriend, a woman who sported a nose ring and hair that was less than a half-inch long, and a plumpish Welsh girl who was the moderator of our discussion.

"I wish they'd send those Bolshies to Cuba," the Welsh girl said. "It's the only place that still buys that tripe."

"I guess you aren't called Maggie for nothing," nose ring put in.

"Oh go on with you," Maggie replied with a dismissive wave of her hand. "I just don't like a person like that to distract us from our purpose."

"And what's that, Maggie?" Gloria asked.

"To expand our minds."

"Right. What do you think about that, Kenny?"

She meant me. But before I could answer, nose ring said, "That's not Kenny. I know Kenny."

Gloria looked at me. I think she was nearsighted. "Aren't you Kenny?"

But before I could reply, the evening's speaker made his appearance and was swamped by the patrons who were anxious to buy him a drink and get some sort of "in." Everyone in the group I was with followed along. Everyone except nose ring.

She was looking at me as if I were quite unusual. This from a person dressed in black leather and studs and a nose ring, and with almost no hair.

"You're not Kenny."

"I never said I was."

"But Gloria said – "

"Gloria must have made a mistake."

Nose ring thought about this a minute and then said, "Well, if you're not Kenny, then who are you and what are you doing here?"

"My name is Michael and I'm a person interested in history."

"You a student?"

I shook my head. "I was a student. I took my degree several years ago."

Nose ring finished her gin and tonic and waved at the barman for another. When she got it, she said, "You talk funny. You're an American, aren't you?"

"Yes." Even with her brain semipickled, she should have been able to figure that one out without asking.

Nose ring screwed up her face. She was trying to give me the evil eye or to consult the spiritual forces that might tell her whether I was to be trusted. "So where are you staying?"

I told her.

"That place's a rip off. Why don't you stay with us?"

"With you?"

"Yeah. You saw our group. We need one more. A guy was supposed to show up last week. His name was Kenny. I was the only one who knew him. But he hasn't shown. And we need the extra money for rent."

What could I say? How do you argue with a nose ring?

The dwelling was a somewhat dilapidated brick row house off Woodstock Road near the Keble College sports ground. The area was somewhat run-down and populated with students who all had bicycles. It was a long walk to the center of the city, so I was able to borrow a bike, provided I put on a new front tire. I did, and found myself riding a bicycle for the first time in fifteen years.

The bicycle gave me a certain feeling of freedom. I could go down lanes cars couldn't. I could lift the bike up on my shoulder and set it in a passageway – no parking problem. And there was never a need for petrol. All in all, I liked the bike situation.

The house had a living room, kitchen, three bedrooms, and a bathroom. It was "furnished" – albeit modified by the students living there. The living room – or sitting room – was an all-purpose room. Aside from the kitchen, it was the only common room in the house.

I learned the name of the nose-ringed girl. It was Q. Not "cue" or "queue" or "kew," but simply Q. She was reading philosophy. Gloria and Peter shared a bedroom and a bed. Maggie and Q shared a bedroom, but had separate beds adjacent to each other. I was in the smallest bedroom. I didn't mind. The rent was a quarter of what I had been paying at the B&B and, with communal grocery shopping and cooking, other expenses were less too.

One day, shortly after I had gotten used to riding my bike, Q asked me if I wanted to ride out to Old Marston.

"What's out there?"

"Nothing much, but it's different from around here."

It sounded like a good thing to me.

Q was a strong rider. She would often get far ahead of me. Though, in all fairness, it should be noted that her bike had gears and mine was a monospeed pedaler.

We took with us a small meal of cheese, sausage, and Bordeaux wine. I carried the backpack on the way out to Old Marston. Q would manage on the way back. We found a grassy bit and set our bikes down. There was a small hill, which we scaled. The early December weather was mild and very comfortable for some exercise. We had no rug so we simply plopped down and broke out the food. I scanned the view above the River Cherwell. It was not a bit of "sportive wood run wild," but it would do.

"You never say much about yourself," Q said.

I nodded. "Neither do you. Neither does anyone."

"You mean Gloria and Peter? They're too much into their own little world to give a damn about anyone else."

I nodded. "Are they engaged or something?"

"More like the 'or something' I'd say. Peter expects that Gloria will marry him after they graduate. But it's my opinion that if he doesn't snare her before then, he'll be out of the running."

"Why's that?"

"Why? Because Gloria's reading economics and has some good contacts. She'll be making twenty or thirty thousand pounds when she gets out, and Peter'll be unemployed. What does she need him for? Lots of lads are keen for a girl who's making thirty thousand as a starting wage."

"Pretty practical, aren't you?"

"I have to be. I'm a philosopher."

I smiled. "Since when is a philosopher practical? I'd have said a philosopher is someone with his head in the clouds."

"That shows how much you know. Ever hear of a bloke named Thales?"

The name seemed vaguely familiar.

"Well, he was a philosopher before the time of Socrates." She lifted her eyebrows.

"I have heard of him," I said with a smile.

"One day he was thinking, and he fell into this well. The people of his village wouldn't get off his back about it so he decided to show them. He calculated the weather for the next year through his star charts. He determined that there would be a bumper harvest, so he took out deposits on all the olive presses he could. When the bumper crop came in he could rent them out at *his* price. He became rich."

"And olive oil was very important in the ancient world."

"It provided oil for lamps, it was the basis for cooking, it was even supposed to make you younger if you rubbed it into your skin."

"A product no one could do without."

"That's right. But Thales wasn't interested in making money. And he didn't care at all about his money. He did it only to make a point: philosophers seem impractical to others because they're not engaged in the mental activity that others are. While others are scheming about how to make another dollar, or how to enhance their careers, philosophers are thinking about problems more basic. More practical."

"What could be more practical than making money?"

"Any proposition that is logically prior to action."

"I don't think I'm following you."

"Say you wanted to be a football player. Wouldn't you say it was more basic to be able to dribble the ball, kick with both feet, head the ball, and so forth?"

"I suppose."

"Then the practical person learns those skills before they attempt to be a football player. It's the same with philosophers. We want to know those propositions that are logically prior to action. While the rest of the world simply assumes its starting points, we attempt to understand them."

"But philosophers never agree on anything. They're working on the same problems they were two thousand years ago."

"It's not the end but the process that's important."

"This is getting a little deep for me," I replied.

Q looked at me with a kind, compassionate expression. I tried to return her gaze, but the sun reflected off her nose ring and made me turn away.

The hardest person in the group to get to know was Maggie Owen. She was fully assembled into her program. Of the whole group, she and Peter seemed most determined to show everyone that they were made of better stuff. They felt they were underappreciated and ought not to have to associate with the likes of us. For example, Maggie used to go on and on with her "Oh, is that what you Americans say . . . do . . . believe . . . ?" I. The American. The bloody American. The bloody typical American. I can speak for all.

Right.

"I've heard that you Americans all own guns."

"I don't own a gun. Therefore, I'm not an American. No. I *am* an American. But perhaps not a *true* American. What is a *true* American?"

"A son-of-a-bitch bent on being the economic ruler of the world."

"Ah, just like our British colonial forefathers."

Cum tacent, clamant.

"Say, aren't you Welsh?"

"What of it?"

"Didn't England do a number on you?"

"I don't know what you're talking about."

"Have you sold out?"

"This is getting ridiculous."

"Is the truth ridiculous?"

"Tertullian said so. Didn't he? 'I believe because it is absurd.'"

"Tertullian didn't love philosophy, did he?"

"What do you have against the Welsh, anyway?"

"The Irish died to free their people."

"The Irish were pigs."

"Yet the Irish are free."

Q: "Let's stay off the Irish. We're both Celts. Why make an issue of it?"

"Darling, this American must know his place."

"Maggie, this American has no place. Haven't you figured that out by now?"

Q's idea of Gloria and Peter was on the mark. One day Peter decided that we all ought to go hear another lecture. I wasn't very keen on it until I heard that the speaker was none other than Hugh Selwyn Mauberley.

"I'm sure that few of you aside from Maggie have ever heard of him," Peter said as he lifted a fried fish finger to his mouth. Gloria looked to Maggie, who was eating a thick potato fry. Gloria didn't like it when Peter made out that the only refined areas were history and literature. Economics was pretty damned important, and if he didn't think so . . .

"Oh really? And what's so important about Mr What's-his-name?"

"It's not related to balance sheets or profits." Peter was talking in his Oxford accent, which was meant to contrast to Gloria's broad working-class accent. "I dare say you wouldn't really appreciate it. Perhaps you'd best stay at home."

"If there weren't people out making the money, then layabouts like you would have to go and get real jobs."

"Now, now," Peter said. The smile was fast disappearing from his face.

"I mean it. The whole scholarly realm is parasitic. It exists only because of the abundance that business has provided for it. Without that abundance, everyone would have to be employed in work that met people's primary needs."

"And what are those primary needs?" Q asked. But she was ignored.

"I'm sure your partner in decadence, Maggie there, would agree with me," Gloria said. "Wouldn't you, Maggie?"

Maggie had her mouth full and was beginning to choke on a fish finger.

"I know who Dr Mauberley is," I suddenly put in. "He teaches at the University of London and his work revolves around the decline of art and the reasons for it."

Everyone stopped. Gloria took her eyes off Peter and Maggie, and stared. Peter dropped some food he was holding and Maggie suddenly stopped choking. The invisible man had spoken.

"Anyone want some more fish fingers?" Q asked.

It was evening. We were riding our bikes to the lecture. I wondered whether I'd see Aisling in the crowd. I wondered what I'd do if I saw her. There was so much I wanted to say that only she would understand. The misting rain splattered on my pants. The bike I was riding had no front fender. The cool temperature was pleasant enough, but the wet chilled me.

We locked our bikes with a common chain and made our way in: Gloria with Peter (holding hands yet apart) and Maggie with Q (not holding hands yet together). I shivered alone.

Inside, the crew found comrades and fashioned themselves into their usual arrangement. I stood at the back awhile, searching the crowd for Aisling. A scrawny pimple-faced boy in a suit gave me a half-page announcement about the talk. *Vocat aestus in umbram.* "The heat calls us into the shade." An odd title.

The speaker was a short man with a few extra pounds around the middle. He was much older than I had pictured. He must have been around sixty or more. I don't see how Ash could have thought he looked like me, unless she had an idea of what I'd look like in years to come.

The little man was almost dwarfed by the lectern. He set in immediately with his theme: "For three years, out of key with his time, he strove to resuscitate the dead art of poetry; to maintain 'the sublime' in the old sense. Wrong from the start!"

During the course of the talk, a mixture of history, philosophy, and literature, Mauberley tried to account for the changes in and failures of literary movements. In the end, he asserted, it was money that was the villain. For money, the artist is tempted to alter his vision to one that will satisfy his audience. (The audience being the one who foots the bill for the whole thing.) But the audience is ignorant of the traditions of literature. The audience wants sex and violence. Alter the formula; change the exposition; it doesn't matter. Create not for your vision but for money. Mauberley depicted this as unnatural usury.

Mauberley claimed that this original sin is described in Aristotle's *Poetics* through the failure to imitate nature. By extension, the work of nature is to supply sustenance to its children since all offspring need nourishment. . . . But usury is to be hated because its gain comes not from nature, but from money itself.

And in Dante *Inferno* XI, 97–111: "Philosophy makes evident through many reasons . . . how all of Nature – her laws, her products and seasons springs from the Greatest Reason . . . but usurers seek their way otherwise. They scorn Nature herself."

"The losers are all of us. All of us as a collection constitute civilization. A civilization corrupted: For an old bitch gone in the teeth, for a botched civilization, for two gross of broken statues, for a few thousand battered books."

When the talk was over, I lingered, remaining in the corner shadows, my back against the wooden paneling. My eyes were open but I saw nothing. It was as if I were emptying out my soul: cleansing it of everything unnatural. An apprehension of nothingness stretched before me. I wanted to understand it.

I walked out of the shadows and back into the room. Someone had left a book under a chair. I went over to pick it up. It was a cheap paperback copy of Donne's poetry. I leafed through it. There was no name. I made my way out and put a note on the college bulletin board with my phone number.

If the owner wanted the book she'd call.

Chapter Fourteen

"Can I come in?"

It was Q. I was lying on my bed reading my newfound book. Poetry really isn't so bad if you read the same poem over and over again. Like a mantra, it seeps inside and becomes a part of you.

Q came over and pulled up a chair. "You know, the Christmas holidays are next week. Do you have any plans?"

I shook my head.

"The reason I was asking was that Maggie's parents have a farm in north Wales. I wanted to go with her, but things are a bit dodgy between her and her parents."

"Dodgy?" I looked at Q. She seemed uncomfortable. Usually she is the unflappable outsider fazed by nothing.

"You know. About Maggie and me. Her parents. Very much old school and all that."

I nodded, though I was not really sure what she was talking about.

"They don't approve of Maggie's lifestyle, and they've never met me . . ."

I had the feeling that I was supposed to make a deduction. But one of the premises seemed to be missing. Q got up from her chair and started pacing the room. Her hands were folded in front of her and she was rubbing her thumbs together.

"So it would be up to you to make things all right," she said.

"All right? I'm not really tracking."

"Don't you see? They have only one spare bedroom. If I go there alone, I'll have to sleep there. And they would be on their guard about me. But if you go along as my boyfriend, then I can sleep with Maggie. Nobody would ever suspect."

I must have appeared quite dull to Q. I had not really thought about their sexual preferences before. So Maggie's parents believed she might be gay, and it was not what they wanted for their daughter. Perhaps they had even gone to lengths to "cure" her of it.

"I don't much like deceiving people."

"Oh, come on, Michael. You wouldn't really be deceiving anyone. You *are* my friend, right?"

"True."

"And you *are* a boy."

"Well, a man. But, yes."

"Then you're my boyfriend."

"False."

"Friend who is a boy; boy who is a friend. This is all semantics, you know. Besides, you'll be helping the cause of true love. Increasing the amount of goodness in the world, as G. E. Moore used to say. What's the harm?"

"I don't like deceiving people, but – "

"Then you'll do it?"

"I don't know."

"Look, you've got nowhere to go on the holidays. Your grant probably doesn't cover that."

"Grant?"

"You are on a grant, aren't you? That's how I've explained your situation to everyone. I mean this is where most of the Americans come when they have a grant. Either here or Cambridge."

"What about the University of London?"

Q made a face. "You aren't serious, are you? You see, I know everything. I know about your grant; I know you don't like being alone by yourself, but you like being alone around others. In Wales you'll be as alone as you please."

I bit my lip. I guess I wouldn't really be hurting anyone. Parents were made to be deceived. Part of the job description.

"Shall I buy a copy of Dylan Thomas?"

"That's south Wales, duckie." And with that she was out of the room. I set my book down. It was a cool day and the window near my bed was covered with condensation. I wrote my name on the pane with my fingertip. Then I imagined that I was Aisling looking at the name "Michael" engraved upon the glass. Such was love's magic that I was transformed. Here you see me, and I am you.

The very image of a name. As soon as it is written, it begins to drip away, to erase itself as the condensation beads to water and the water drips to the sill, my name is erased from your eyes forever.

But this is idle talk. The words of the old, the sick, and the dying.

Eluned and Glyn Owen ran a farm just outside Conwy. It was near the edge of the Snowdonia National Park. They grew vegetables and raised sheep as primary occupations. In addition, Eluned did some sewing and ran a bed-and-breakfast in the summer, and Glyn was a barn carpenter during the winter. All in all, they were a family of frugal habits. This set their expenses well below their income. Their son was an engineer working in Toronto. Maggie was the younger by fifteen years.

"We had two children. One at a time," Eluned said with a sly smile.

Glyn was a man of few words. The first love of his life were his sheepdogs. They were allowed in the house and slept in a room that contained the television and Mr Owen's favorite chair. There was also a foldout bed on which the Owens slept in the summer. This gave them an extra room to let for the B&B and also afforded them the comfort of being on the lower level, which was cooler in the summer (being partially built into the hill). There was a stone fireplace in that room – one of four in the house. Eogue would have winced at the simplicity of the Owens' practical mantelpieces.

The farmhouse was situated on a hill (as were most of the houses in this rolling terrain). It had been added to a number of times in the last 150 years since its construction, when it replaced a two-hundred-year-old house destroyed in a fire.

Walking around the town of Conwy, I got the feeling that I was mingling with a conquered people. First, there was the castle built by Edward in his conquest of Wales nine hundred years before. Second, most of the people spoke Welsh; they understood English well enough, but among themselves they spoke Welsh. A sign of an independent people is when they maintain their own language. Third, was their way of referring to the English as if they were a different race. And indeed the Welsh looked different from the English, in their hair and skin color. Two sorts of hair color prevailed: jet black and light brown (with a hint of red). This was mixed with pale white skin or ruddy, Irish-looking skin. The features were not as harsh or as big as those of the English, but rather more subtle – like their culture, which had had to exist in secret throughout much of their occupied history. This secrecy was expressed in many ways. One way was the long Welsh names, such as the traditional: Gwilym ap Sion ap Emrys ap Dafydd ap Owain ap Hywel ap Rhodri ap Rhydderch ap Gryffyd. The name bespoke the pedigree of the speaker (though in modern times the names were shortened). There was no alienating oneself from one's kin or blood. The relationship was dark, deep, and everlasting.

I was anxious that our little "secret" not be found out. Q had held my hand when we were introduced to the Owens. She turned her head to me and gazed longingly as if I were her heartthrob. For my part, I did nothing. A boyfriend who was aloof and undemonstrative would certainly raise no eyebrows. I felt I was holding up my end.

I imagined that the Owens – particularly Eluned – would have their ears to the doors listening to whether Q would come into my room at night. They struck me as people who liked to know what was happening under their roof. They were nobody's fools.

Q didn't come to me in the night, of course. But in Maggie's room, there *was* a bit of noise, and it didn't take Sherlock Holmes to figure out what was going on. I wondered how and whether this discovery would be brought to light.

It was December, but there was no snow. Often the snow wouldn't come until January or February. "It's the global warming. That's what it is," Eluned declared one evening during dinner.

Dinner was a time when Eluned would unload whatever happened to be on her mind. Mrs Owen's version of honesty was to speak without restraint. Glyn would leave when he had had enough of this.

"So do you know any nice boys at the university, Maggie?" Eluned asked during dinner one evening. Because there were guests, English was being spoken.

"Oh yes. Several."

"And what might their names be?"

"Angelo and Rodrigo."

Mrs Owen took a helping of potatoes and chewed them more than necessary. "Are there no Welsh boys at Oxford?"

"I'm sure there are."

Mr Owen pushed his plate forward. He had finished.

"Well?" Eluned asked suggestively.

"Mother, I didn't go to university to meet boys."

"Oh, I suppose you had a more practical idea in mind. Like studying Milton. Some English poet."

"Milton was a great poet, mother."

"There were great Welsh poets, too. But they're never taught in the English schools. But that's not my point. You'll never get a job from all your studying of Milton."

"You want me to become an engineer and move to Toronto?"

"There are always jobs for engineers."

"You want me to move to Toronto?"

"I want you to find a husband. Your father and I won't be able to support you forever."

With that, Glyn left the room. But Eluned wasn't finished.

"I don't know how to light the fire in your belly, girl. It just seems like you have no ambition."

"I work hard at my studies."

"That's not what I mean and you know it."

I decided that it was time to excuse myself, too. I went in search of Glyn. I found him outside, smoking a pipe. The stars were out as they could be only in the country. They lent a structure to things that seemed as mysterious as it was powerful.

"Beautiful country," I said after standing next to the man for a few minutes. Glyn was leaning against a fence post watching one of his dogs trot in from some adventure.

"They have no country like this in America," I ventured.

"I should think not," was his reply.

"Mind you, they have *other* country. It has its own power. The area around where I was born, in the Midwest, is basically flat. Good for growing maize. Thousands of acres of it. Amazing."

"These hills are for families, not businessmen."

Now it was my turn to be silent. At this time of year there weren't many night birds. But it could have been that my eyes weren't accustomed to seeing in the dark of a country sky. I turned and studied Glyn. He was interacting with the environment in a private way. Though he seemed impassive, I could sense that more was going on. I decided that I should leave him alone.

"These mountains hold things in. It's the way of the land," Glyn said as I turned away.

"Yes. The land."

"It tells you what will be. It controls you. A lot of people never understand that. They come in with their pamphlets from

London telling us how to control the land. 'Increase your yields,' they say. Some of my neighbors went in for it. I say, 'What's it like with it and without it?' Unless you can show me that my life is better with it, I don't see a reason to change. And I'm not just talking about taking in more crops, neither."

I was beyond my depth.

"It's no good to get more unless there's a reason for it. There's always a payback."

"A payback," I repeated, nodding.

"Simple as that," he said knocking out his pipe. He had said what he had to say to me.

I thought about Glyn and Eluned and their natural ordering of things. I thought also about their daughter Maggie and of Q. I wondered if the Owens knew what the two young women were up to and I wondered if their lesbian relationship, too, had a place in the natural order.

Their life was a hard one. It was not to be romanticized. But they lived with few unfulfilled desires. The stars. The weather. The mountains. These determined their desires. Not Madison Avenue.

Christmas in the Owen residence was unlike any I had ever experienced. I had been tutored by Maggie on how it would be, but I was unprepared for the effect it would have on me. In my family, we had always celebrated Christmas by observing both the pagan solstice festival and the Christian remembrance of the birth of the baby Jesus. The two of these often collided. For, centered on the solstice festival was the theme of "a year ended." Similar to the annual profit-sharing bonus, we also shared in our bounty by giving to others. We were obliged, literally, to take of the material goods that had been given to us and to return these in some fashion to *others*. Now who these "others" were was left to personal interpretation. The common myth was that we gave small presents to the immediate family and also to the poor and needy, the fire department, the police department, the Society for the Prevention of Cruelty to Animals, the Society for the

Prevention of Cruelty to the Red-spotted Snapping Turtle, and other such deserving groups.

Then there were the token gifts – to secretaries and the like, which meant we deserved some sincere thanks even though the amount of the gift was less than an hour of real pay to them. It was the *thought* that counted. The fact that these people were even in our thoughts showed our noblesse oblige. The token gifts became a heap. No one liked or cared for them. Most were tossed away or destroyed or neglected. What a waste, except for the merchants who had stores that specialized in "gifts-that-really-don't-count-for-a-damn." In the new cathedrals that had been popping up across America – the shopping malls – the gifts-that-really-don't-count-for-a-damn stores were definitely a growth industry.

Then there was the splurge gift. The gift that really let people know that we were sacrificing for them. Perhaps one of the starred items in the Boston Museum of Fine Arts Catalogue.

My moronic reaction to last Christmas had failed to produce the desired effect. Perhaps the mold was flawed. How can a religion that says that the gateway to heaven is barred to the rich encourage such largesse – unless it is giving the big rollers an opportunity to part with their worldly baggage so that they, too, might enter the heavenly kingdom. Kind of like selling an indulgence. Plop go the money-changing tables.

The Owens' Christmas was different from that of many Britons. First, they went to religious services. This marked them off, to be sure. The service moved at an unhurried pace. It was not the bristling military discipline so often displayed or aspired to in the State Church, but was rather a deceptively informal gathering.

Second, there was no Christmas tree.

Now, I've always been ambivalent about the Christmas tree. I'd heard that most people in Britain still observed the German (né Saxon) custom of killing the one variety of tree that keeps its chloroplasts operating continually. But I've always wondered about the reason for doing this. Is it about showing eternal life through the coniferous tree? But isn't this negated when we kill the symbol of eternal life and set it on display? Such confusion gives me a headache.

Third, each person was limited to giving a single gift – and only then to someone of their blood. (Thus there was to be no exchange between the Owens and their houseguests, though we were allowed to exchange gifts with each other.) And, generally, the single gift was something the gift giver already had; therefore that person was parting with what he or she already had in order to give to another. His or her loss was your gain: a singular presentation – not many, but precious. *Pauca sed bona*.

Finally, there was the Christmas dinner, which was a goose accompanied by a dish prepared by each of the guests. We all took our turns. I prepared a sort of Cos salad (not the most challenging project in the world).

The exchange of goods resulted in my giving to Q the cap that I wore (an Oxford country tweed variety) and getting from her a thin volume of Zen writings. All in all, I think I liked this form of gift exchange.

At the table, we each passed around the dishes we'd prepared, and everyone was obliged to sample a bit of everything. Q had made a strange semisweet brown paste that was supposed to be eaten with black bread. Since we had no true black bread, she had made a pumpernickel variant with the effect that it was not tough enough to bring out the real character of the paste.

The conversation revolved around the Owen family's past gatherings. It was at the end of one chain of remembrances, about a male relative, that Maggie broke in.

"But what's the point of Uncle Evan sacrificing everything for his family. Look, the man had a double first in Classics as well as competencies in philosophy. He was lined up for a key post with the Foreign Secretary. But just because his father killed himself, the bloke comes home and tries to run the family business."

"And a noble act it was, too," Eluned said.

"Noble nothing. It was sheer stupidity," Maggie returned.

"What's stupid about taking care of your own?" her mother said, pursing her lips and raising her chin.

"He sacrificed his god-given gifts. I'd say that's a sin."

"Is it a sin to look after your blood?"

"In Wales, blood is all there is. But should a person become nothing just to support his blood?"

"How is someone nothing if he has supported his blood?"

"What about his own happiness?"

"Fine and good if it can happen without sacrificing one's duty."

"There you go again. Where is your duty? I say your duty is to yourself."

At this Glyn stirred. He was ready to leave. But before he did, he uttered the only words I had heard come from his lips at the dinner table the entire time I stayed with the Owens. "And who are you? Are you anything apart from your blood?" The old farmer struck himself upon his breast with his fist.

With that, he left.

The spell had been broken. The texts and the subtexts of dialogue resonated within the stonewalled house.

Chapter Fifteen

"I knew this was a mistake." Q said. We were walking up the Owens' road to help digest our dinner. It was a cold night and Q had on no coat, only a woolen sweater.

"Their fighting has nothing to do with you."

Q said nothing, but pursed her lips and shook her head.

We walked along the one-lane road. The moon was out so that there was adequate light for walking. "Glyn moves according his own rules," I ventured.

"Hell's bells. He's just a crotchety old man. There's nothing mysterious about him," Q said.

"I don't know. He seems so unaffected by the forces of society."

"Which society? British society of the twentieth century? That's true. The man lives in eleventh-century Wales. No. I'm not about to canonize the likes of that. It's they who oppress the likes of me. They've no tolerance. Zero. I'll tell it to you straight, Michael. Maggie's got to make a clean break of it. Like her brother. Unless she does, those parents of hers are going to drive her to suicide."

"What do *you* want?"

"I want Maggie. But I'll give her up unless she quits putting me through all this crap. *Nobody's* worth this."

"Nobody?" I asked. Q didn't respond. I thought about her pain. I thought about her rigid standards. If only she'd ease up. If only she didn't want so much from people. Her pain seemed to be in direct proportion to her desire that everything be just as she imagined it should be. Eliminate the desire, and you eliminate the pain at not fulfilling that desire. But at what cost? As Glyn had said, there's payback for everything.

We walked a little farther, but I was getting cold – even with a coat. "Do you still want to take that walk tomorrow, up Snowdon?"

Q saw that I was turning around, but she still had things to work over. "We'll climb the mountain and then we'll cut out of here. I can't stand it any longer."

When I got to my room, I picked up the book Q had given me. It was a thin clothbound volume of only fifty pages or so entitled *The Book of Mu*. The old blue binding was showing signs of deterioration. It was a collection of stories and poems.

I read a story before going to sleep. It was about the nun Chiyono, who studied Zen under Bukko of Engaku. Chiyono searched for understanding, but was unable to find enlightenment. All her thinking; all her trials, everything seemed for naught. She felt as if she were getting nowhere. Then, one moonlit night, she was carrying water in an old pail bound with bamboo. The bamboo broke and the bottom fell out of the pail. At that moment, Chiyono understood. She was free!

To commemorate the event she wrote this poem:

In this way and that I tried to save the old pail
Since the bamboo strip was weakening and about to break
Until at last the bottom fell out.
No more water in the pail!
No more moon in the water!

I imagined Aisling reading that story. I thought about the letters that she and I had exchanged (more on her side than on mine), and about the letter I would write to her when it was time.

"Are you sure you want to do this?" I asked as we approached the mountain.

Maggie looked at me as if I were a weakling. "What's the matter? Too much soft American living? In Wales it's deep in our blood. The wind howls. The temperature drops. It only makes us more determined."

I couldn't help but think of Maggie's parents. What was there about Welsh blood, anyway?

It wasn't as if I didn't think myself up to the task – though the thought of hiking straight up for half a day in the cold was rather daunting. To add to the mystery, the mountain was enveloped in fog, so we had a view only of the lower half of the mountain. I never liked going somewhere I knew nothing about. The unknown frightened me.

On the other hand it was sunny. And sun – even on a cold day – can lift my spirits beyond compare. It would probably burn off the fog before we got there.

Glyn had lent us his car and it had taken us well over an hour to reach the base of the mountain. From there it was a steady, steep path to the summit of one of the highest mountains in the British Isles. Everything we needed on our hike was in a single rucksack, which Q was carrying now but that we would shift among us.

Maggie and Q seemed to be reconciled for the time being and were chatting amicably while I followed along behind. I had not bothered to stay in shape since I'd stopped coaching, and the physical exertion was beginning to take its toll. We had walked for only a half hour when I was ready for a rest.

"Just ten more minutes," Maggie promised. She seemed to be getting stronger as the hike continued.

"Ten minutes," I returned. The cold air burned my lungs. I wished I had brought a walking stick as Maggie and Q had.

After twenty minutes, I sat down. I felt I could go no farther. Maggie and Q didn't seem to notice that I had stopped. They were in their own world. The fog line was close. The sun was

Michael Boylan

not burning it off. The fog seemed to be in motion about the mass of rock.

From where I was sitting I could see down into a deep valley. The drop-off must have been at least three hundred feet. Suddenly, I felt scared – scared that I might slip and fall, scared that someone might push me, scared that I might jump.

I got up and resumed walking. The boots that Mr Owens had lent me for the climb were too big and even though I had put on three pairs of socks, I still felt a dozen or so blisters forming on my feet. This was no easy hike. A person could get hurt up here.

Soon I was into the fog. It wasn't merely cutting my vision but also misting rain. It seemed to be another world. I imagined I was going back in time to the Wales before Edward's conquest. This was a Wales where the rugged landscape kept people like the Owens in their own part of the world their entire lives. When people would not wander beyond a dozen miles from their homes, no farther than they could walk in a day over rough terrain.

How would such people see a mountain like this? Would they want to climb it? Why was I climbing it? Why had I read the zen story about the pail, the water, and the moon? Something had driven me to it. Was it my own tattered worldview that was ready for collapse?

Or was it something else? Was it desire itself? Certainly complete lack of desire is death. For then, we'd do nothing. Surely this was not the answer. Yet desire seemed also to be at the center of many evils. It is false that money is the root of evil. For money has no power, aside from the power we give it ourselves. It is not money but our attitude toward money that is at fault. Our fear of poverty is largely groundless, too, since other evils may befall us that seem terrible because we make them so. Our attitudes toward them create the evil in them. These attitudes cause us to assume burdens that are with us forever.

As I followed the trail – now snow-covered – alone in the mist I felt myself to be upon another journey. It was a journey that had begun when my father died. Maybe before. Maybe it began when I had to make decisions about what direction my life would take. When I decided on teaching in a rich suburb rather than at the inner-city school in which I'd done my student teaching.

But this was beside the point of my inner journey. If I knew the direction, then the rest would no longer matter. If I knew the direction, then my way would be clear to me.

It was important that I hike alone. It was important that only gravity be my guide. I had to find my own way. This was an ascent that was uniquely my own and that I could never explain to anyone.

When I reached the summit I looked around for Maggie and Q. Visibility was still poor. The winds were gusting and causing the mist to cut sharp into your skin, like fine needles.

Suddenly I heard a familiar voice, "Where were you? We're hungry." It was Q. They were coming down off a twelve-foot boulder that others had been scaling, too.

"You could have gone ahead and eaten. I wouldn't have minded." I said the words before I realized that it had been my shift with the backpack. I had forgotten about my load.

Maggie's nose was running but she didn't seem to mind; she was intent on relieving me of my burden.

"You've got to climb the rock over there. That's the official summit," Q said.

I nodded.

"Go ahead. We won't eat your food," Maggie said.

I turned to the boulder.

"Mind the damp. It's slippery."

 I climbed up the final boulder and stood atop Mount Snowdon. I could see nothing. There was the same wind and mist as before. There was very little difference up here, save the recognition that this was the real peak. Officially, I was now at the top. But I had already reached a summit.

Part Four

Chapter Sixteen

The Book of Mu Continued

Siddhartha spent the next six years of his life as a sadhu. He actively sought the *atman* through rigorous discipline and self-control. His fame grew far and wide and many sadhus came and sought him out. Through great fasting and denial Siddhartha experienced visions. This is not unlike other religious leaders who have done the same. One is reminded of St Jerome in the Christian tradition, as well as the many mystics like St John of the Cross or St Bernard. Hafiz, the Moslem poet, proclaimed that mystical love with God was like loving a woman.

But of course, Siddhartha's visions may only have been a result of his not eating. It has been this author's experience that fasting brings about visions. Are these visions insights into reality or merely the chemical misfiring of a nutritionally impoverished brain?

Siddhartha had the same misgivings. One day he saw a young milkmaid. She had just milked a cow and was returning home with the warm milk in a wooden bowl.

Siddhartha viewed the maid from the opposite bank of a small river. He jumped into the water, swam across, and presented himself before the maid without saying a word.

The maid took pity on the emaciated man and offered him the milk. Siddhartha accepted. He downed it readily, and when the milk reached his stomach, Siddhartha realized that the way of self-denial is *not* the way to awakening.

I shut the book for a moment. I thought about Siddhartha's situation. He had tried luxury and voluntary poverty. Neither had worked. I could agree with that. Neither had worked for me, either (though I had gotten the order reversed and my poverty hadn't been nearly as intense, nor had it been voluntary).

I turned for a moment back to the "Ode to Empty."

> I'm sure the moment at which I died and when
> I became aware I was dead, were distinct,
> And separate, with the former preceding, then
> Causing the latter – slowly sinking
> Into my brain, through the *think*
> To rot the *I*: radical transcendental.
> I thought that you were life
> I worshipped reason and pledged you all
> My soul thinking music and philosophy
> Were all that mortal man could ever hope to see
> But my supreme, imperious "I" did fall
> When something greater than my subjective
> Majesty proved to be, instead of me, the all
> And mighty leveler of subjects to eternity.

> And in this
> I become free
> To finally see, I stumble blindly
> And mark my life in finitude.
> Oh mu, oh empty,
> Oh blinding light
> Which first I knew before my birth
> In a blue stench
> Your putrid rises to my head
> As I, now on what was
> Dead to me, but
> Now

More alive in being connected to
A nothingness.

Again, I shut the book. This was getting intense for me. I decided to turn back to Siddhartha.

When Siddhartha realized that both pleasure and asceticism were really two sides of the same coin, he was ready to awaken. But Mara, the god of death, was rather upset that Siddhartha might have uncovered his secrets and plied Siddhartha with many temptations, ending in his stark revelation of his morbid self.

Siddhartha withstood even this final test – except that it wasn't the final test. There was still one more avenue to explore. Many readers might ask, why not stay by yourself forever? The enlightened one needs nobody else. (This may remind many readers of Plato's "Allegory of the Cave.")

The Buddha had now emerged. He would return to the world, though he might appear ridiculous. He would return because it was his duty to do so. He would return to the world to teach others, and he taught for the next forty-five years.

Once more I closed the book. I thought about my own life. I may not have been totally enlightened, but things had changed for me. My experiments were over. It was time to re-enter the world.

> My days of running are now long past
> For though I can sometimes move quickly,
> I cannot move with the same wild and free
> Abandon that once lifted me high as
> Though on a fertile, green mountain peak cast
> Upwards in the dialects of human
> Understanding. Because now I can see
> That the mountain without life supporting
> Its sides would gradually be torn
> Away by the elements and the green dorred
> To a deathly blue. Just as waxen wings
> Must always melt, so wild notions of the mastery

Of what is, *is* only the towering babbling
Of an idiot and signifies nothing.
The limit of matter is light and of life
Dying. Not that my music is no longer
Beauty, for that never changes, in purity
And grace, and but for philosophy
I would not lie prostrate cognizant of error
In thought – yet what I now sense in song
Is occasioned by the possibility of not being –
A terror too real to be real
For to be is to see,
And in emptiness there is nothing
No nothing
Emptiness
empty

         mu.

January 1, 1992

Dear Aisling,

I would like to come by to see you if it is convenient.

I have many things to tell you. But it seems that writing them down does not work very well for me. I have written this letter several times and thrown each draft away. The thoughts I have had are not easily expressed on paper.

I'm not sure whether this is a fault of the thoughts or of my inability to express them. I have been searching for other modes of insight and other ways to express myself. Yes, I have been reading some poetry. It seems to me that in poetry there is often some sort of emblem that becomes

        Michael Boylan

the focus of the poem. Our thoughts dance around this image through the application of the poetic devices. The more the reader knows about them, the more he is able to travel away from the central principle to other supporting routes. At the same time, there is the self-conscious beauty of the whole thing. The poem is so very stylized. This means that both the music and the image capture you immediately. Afterward, the other parts of the map may reveal themselves to the reader.

The truth of this revelation is not in the beauty *per se*, but in our reflection on the interrelation between image and music. The truth occurs in us. We discover it. Either the revealed truths square with the way we think things are or they do not. Only the truths that correspond seem important to us. Ultimately, it is these truths that inform and change our psyches.

Poetry is thus indirect. Philosophy and science are direct. They set out their truths into propositions that fit into arguments. These arguments are judged to be valid or invalid according to strict rules of inference. The truths of the premises themselves are often judged according to how they correspond to empirical reality (as commonly experienced by some group of people).

Religion and narrative fiction fall between. It seems they aspire to one pole or the other depending upon how scientific or poetic they wish to be. Is the message to be directly in the word or story, or in the interpretation of the same? If the latter, then how do you construct road signs to guide your reader to your destination? Buddha said that the path to salvation is a traceless path upon which no two people travel.

Interpretation is thus by nature subjective: a composition that you put together in your own way. The question remains, "How do you know when you've got it?" The disquieting answer to this is that there are no clear criteria.

How are you doing on your dissertation? What is your job like? Is it likely to be renewed for next year? These and other practical questions form one part of my mind. Yet what I really want to do is to talk about metaphysics. Please write me if this is all right.

Yours,
Michael

I posted the letter as soon as I had returned to Oxford. I waited for a month with no response.

February 10, 1992

Dear Aisling,

> Whilst yet to prove
> I thought there was some Deitie in love,
> So did I reverence, and gave
> Worship; as Atheists at their dying houre
> Call, what they cannot name, an unknown power,
> As ignorantly did I crave:
> Thus when
> Things not yet knowne are coveted by men,
> Our desires give them fashion, and so
> As they waxe lesser, fall, as they rise, grow.

Is the poet sincere when he bids farewell to love? Is this just a pose – a rhetorical question that is ironically meant to indicate the opposite? How is it that we understand irony? And if it is not understood, is irony simply lying?

Please send me word.
Michael

Yet still I had no word.

Things at the house were beginning to run their course. Gloria was working hard for her finals. She had a top job lined up, and everyone could see that as far as Gloria was concerned, Peter was history. (Everyone except Peter, that is.) Poor Peter couldn't see that he had played his hand badly and that he would have to take his seventeenth-century English History degree and file it neatly on a shelf somewhere and find himself a real job.

Peter was not talented enough to go on in history. He could have attached himself to a real star in Gloria, but he had been so intent on assuming a preeminent role that he had lost her altogether.

One day in early April, he tried to bring things to a head. It was a Thursday and several people in his crowd were going into London for the weekend. Peter was busy in his role of executive manager (i.e., arranging Gloria's schedule for her).

"But you'll have to do it tonight if we're to leave by early afternoon. You have something or other in the morning, don't you?"

"I'm not going on your holiday. I have to meet the people at Chambers and Turrow."

"But that's just in the morning. You can finish that off by two or so. Then we can pop down in your car to Wilfred's place in Chelsea. Frightfully lush, they say." Peter shut his eyes soulfully as he considered the tremendous enjoyment of being at an expensive town house while the aged parents who owned it were away. The hedonistic possibilities were endless.

"Why don't you go yourself. You don't need me."

Gloria was peeling potatoes for some soup. The carrots and tomatoes were already in the pot. All that remained were the potatoes, spices, and the broth from last night's chicken. Peter stood alongside her – close enough for his presence to be felt but far enough away so as not to get splattered by the cooking.

He sighed, "You don't understand. You *must* go."

Gloria didn't respond. She trimmed the last potato and began adding the chicken stock to the pot.

Now it was time to talk tough. Peter grabbed Gloria's arm hard and spun her around. She spilled some of the stock. Her eyes were cold even as his were hot.

"Listen, bitch. You'll do as I goddamn tell you."

Gloria freed her arm and in one motion turned the flame up on the soup. With her task completed, she took off her apron and tossed it to the floor. "You can't talk to me that way," she said.

"I'll talk to you any friggin' way I choose. You're my woman." Peter's voice had dropped his affected Oxford accent. He again grabbed Gloria by the shoulders and tried to pull her to him.

Gloria pushed her arms against his chest, freeing herself once again. "I'm not your woman. Keep your hands off me, Peter. I don't want you anymore."

"What is it about this job, anyway? They throw some money at you and instantly you're married to it: typical economics business mentality. Think of me for once. Think of your responsibilities!"

"Goodbye, Peter," she said with a controlled smile.

Then she pivoted and headed for the stairs.

"I'm not finished yet," Peter said. The words had no effect. "I'm not finished. Gloria! I'm not finished," Peter lunged after her, but she was a better escape artist than he was a jailer. He was left with nothing but air.

It wasn't until Gloria had left the room that he became aware of the rest of us watching him. "Damn bitch. I'll straighten her out," he said.

"Sure you will," Q intoned with a smile.

Peter left the house. He wasn't back for dinner. He went on his trip, but when he returned he found that Gloria had gone. She had arranged to move into a room in her college, recently vacated by a student who had dropped out. Her intention was to curtail her social life and concentrate on studying. Our paths were unlikely to cross again. She sent a friend with a van to pick up her things from the house and deliver a goodbye note and a check for her last month's rent.

"Very decent of her to do this," Q said as she drew the check from the envelope.

Peter had other ideas. He was a changed man. His swagger and hauteur had left him and he was drinking rather heavily. One day in May, a man named Miles came by to see him. I was the lucky one who opened the door.

"Is this the residence of Peter Wickham?" the man asked. He was rather squarish, with bushy eyebrows and a prominent jaw. I was instantly reminded of Mr Tweed, the lawyer who had represented Sara.

"Why do you want to know?" I replied.

"Can I come in?"

"I'd rather talk to you out here."

"Have it your way. I can bring the lot of you into this if you don't cooperate."

"Cooperate with what? You still haven't told me why you're here."

The man laughed. As he did so, his jaw moved forward and back. It reminded me of a bulldog's. "Oh, you'll be seeing a lot of me. I can tell you. Near the end of the term. Them's the type what will skip out on their responsibilities."

"Does he owe you money?"

"Does he owe me money? He's four months late on one bill and three months late on another." The man waved some papers in the air.

"Have you tried to contact him at college?"

"They won't help. 'Not their problem,' they say. Damned if it isn't everybody's problem when people go skipping out on their responsibilities. Thinks I won't go after him for eighty pounds, but that's where he's wrong. I'd go after him for 80p, I would. You can tell him that if he doesn't pay, I'm going to make life a living hell for him. The middle of the night, anytime. I'll be around until my bill is paid. I don't care who pays it, but it will be paid. I will have my money."

Peter wasn't at dinner, but I brought the subject up in his absence.

"Kick him out," Maggie said. "The man's going down fast."

"I say we pay his bill," Q returned. "It's been rather hard on him, what with Gloria leaving him and all."

"He deserved *that*."

"I don't care what he deserved. It's still quite a blow."

"She would have left even if he hadn't been so keen to show off his phony aristocratic airs. Gloria never worked on 'fixing' *her* accent. Peter was in love with *his*. Trying to make everyone believe he was from an elite family."

"He does have some blue blood on his mother's side."

"But no money. No title and no money. You can brag about your blue blood all you want, but the fact is, your blue blood *alone* won't get the cows milked any earlier." Maggie was very resolute. I had a feeling that there was another agenda to the two women's discussion, which wasn't my business.

I resolved to find Peter and talk with him.

I found him in the pub where I had first met Gloria. He was sitting with a group of younger students. They were laughing over empty glasses. Peter looked serious, and he was drinking too much. Liquor not beer. Straight not mixed. His eyes were clouded, but his gaze was fixed.

"Peter, I need to talk with you a moment." With some difficulty I extracted him from the group and got him outside. I went over the part about the bill collector and the fact that we rarely saw Peter at the house anymore.

"The fact is, old son, I'm moving out of that bloody house. I haven't got my gear together yet, but I will. Soon. So you can tell that to the gemini sisters and get the hell out of my life."

I didn't ask about his share of the rent. I knew he didn't have it.

Peter went his own way. He eventually had some friends pick up his things. They came by while only I was there. I bet Peter had that timed. He knew that Maggie wouldn't have let them in.

Whenever Miles came by (and he did come by, often), I told him that Peter had left. I even showed him around the house. But the man figured that it was all part of a clever ruse. What finally made a believer of him was an episode in which he made an evening visit. The man was convinced that he would catch us at our "hiding Peter" scheme. He entered the house without knocking and proceeded to carry out his own inspection of the place. When he got to Q and Maggie's bedroom, he found the two of them *in naturalibus*.

He had discovered a secret, all right, but the wrong one. Miles was finally convinced that what we had to hide was not Peter.

Occasionally, I saw Peter around town. Sometimes in a pub. Sometimes in a park. Sitting by himself. Drinking from an ill-disguised bottle. Morning, noon, and night. Peter Wickham was always tight.

He never even took his exams. And before the end of June, he was nowhere to be found. Too many bill collectors. Too little studying. Too much booze. But he still retained his Oxford accent.

Chapter Seventeen

I ran into Aisling by chance.

I had just bought some groceries at the small shop down the block. Whenever we properly shopped, that is, for several days or more worth of groceries, we would take the bus to the Sainsbury's supermarket two miles away. Supermarket shopping was a group effort, since there were multiple bags to carry. But whenever we couldn't or wouldn't go to Sainsbury's, we went to the little shop instead, because it was more convenient, only a quarter mile from the house. It was also much more costly, but the Pakistani couple who ran it were rather friendly, so I preferred going there.

It was near the end of June. When the month was over we would be leaving our house. Maggie had gotten a job at an independent school in Yorkshire, and Q was staying in Oxford, where she would increase the hours in her job at a small publishing house.

It was my turn to make dinner. I had decided upon soup and bread. I didn't have the energy for Sainsbury's so I had gone for a walk to the little store. It was around seven in the evening – still very light out – only the brightness had dimmed. I had just gotten out of the store with my small bundle when I saw a figure that caused me to pause. To this day I don't know what it was that made me hesitate. I focused my attention on the figure approaching.

It was Aisling.

I felt paralyzed. A million contradictory emotions ran through me. I started and stopped, then started again. As I walked toward her, I increased my pace until I was running. Aisling saw me. She stopped where she was and waited for me to reach her.

"Aisling!" I managed when I had stopped. I was holding my parcel of groceries, breathless.

"Well, it's about time," she said with a smile.

There were so many things I wanted to talk about. All at once. I felt the beads of sweat rolling off my forehead and onto the thin plastic bag that held my groceries. "What are you doing here?"

"In Oxford? In Britain? In general?" She tilted her head to one side. This playfulness. I had forgotten all about her playfulness. So many details had slowly receded from my mind in the year and three quarters since I had seen her. Her light brown hair was longer than it had been in Bethesda. But the fair skin and the freckles that seemed to dance when she smiled were just as I remembered them.

"Let's go somewhere. Let's talk. Are you busy? Is it all right?"

"As you can see, I'm engaged," she said with a serious tone.

"Engaged?" my voice almost cracked. I swallowed hard.

"Engaged in a walk to the store. Serious business these walks," she said, slowly raising her left hand to her chin and then cocking her head to the side.

"There's a bench. Let's sit down before I drop these groceries."

"Good idea. I wouldn't want to be the cause of your wasting food."

So we sat on the bench. Aisling on one end. Me on the other. The bag in between us. I couldn't take my eyes off her. I didn't realize how much she captivated me. I had been away from her so long.

"So tell me. Why are you in Oxford?" I said.

"I'm living here. Have been since the beginning of the term," she replied.

"Since the beginning of the term?"

"That's right. Just down the block from where you're living."

"What! You've known where I've been living and you haven't come to see me?" Suddenly I felt completely off-balance. What was she saying? Why was she saying it? When did she find out I was in Oxford? How did she?

"You remember the talk by Dr Mauberley?"

I nodded. She was calling him Dr Mauberley now. Was that important? I didn't dwell on it. "But I looked around the room for you that night and I didn't see you," I said.

"Then you didn't look hard enough." She looked away and paused before she spoke again, "Actually, you did scan the room. I saw you doing that. But you were so keen on the weird menagerie of undergraduates you had with you that you didn't scan the halls outside. In fact, I was standing in the doorway. A little late, perhaps, but I was there, nonetheless. In fact, I stood there for about a third of the lecture."

"You in the doorway. There all the time?"

"You simply didn't look behind you. You were only intent on the newness of everything, I suppose. Though I did leave you a calling card," she said with a smile.

I paused. "The book under the chair? That was you? Sometimes coincidences mean something, I suppose. I can't believe how I could have missed you."

"We all miss people in our own ways, Michael," Ash said, extending her hand and lightly touching my face. "I knew from your notes that you were in England. I had also figured out that you were unhappy, by the manner and number of your letters."

"I'm not a very good letter writer. Not a good writer, period."

"You might say I was curious. I was curious about what was happening to you. Why you were in England, and what you were doing with your life."

"But why didn't you come and see me?"

"Your letter sounded like the epistle of a disturbed man. If I intervened and came to you first, I felt that I might harm you. But I couldn't just stay away. I taught during the fall and got a temporary post doing some research here so I could be near you. It also made it easier for me to finish my dissertation."

"You've finished?"

She nodded. I grabbed both of her hands to congratulate her. It was not enough. I slid over and kissed her on the lips. How I had missed those lips. But now the memory came back to me completely. I felt a rise of joy.

"Ash, I'm so happy for you. I'm so excited."

"I finished in early May and I defend it next week."

"Is it open to the public? Can I come?"

She shook her head. "Technically they're public, but in practice it's just me and my committee and any fellow graduate students who are still writing. Though I'm hoping none of them will show up because they'll be expected to ask questions, and the fewer of those I have to deal with, the better. It will be in London. Closed doors and all that." Then she lifted her eyebrows. "But outside those doors they do have seats."

I kissed her again and would probably have kept on kissing her if I hadn't knocked over my bag of groceries. The thin plastic bag split open and the ingredients for dinner spilled out all over the ground.

I laughed from the depth of my belly. "Well, you said you've been waiting for a sign. That's it. Help me gather this up, and in return you can have my famous vegetable soup."

"I didn't know you had a recipe for vegetable soup."

"Sure I do. Got it from the lady at the little store. Tonight will be its world premiere. Want to be there?"

"I think I'd better. Should you warn the others at your house?"

"No. Let it be a surprise. Tonight is a night for surprises!"

Maggie and Q greeted me with hostility. "We thought you'd gone over with Peter," Maggie said.

"Decide to grow your own vegetables instead of buying them at the store?"

"Ladies, I'd like to introduce you to a friend of mine, Aisling Dunnegan."

The two looked up in a hurry. They had not even noticed Aisling standing there. "Irish, then, are you?" Q asked.

"Q here is Irish, and Maggie is Welsh," I said completing the introductions.

"Actually, I'm an American, just like Michael. But as you can tell by my name, I do have Irish ancestors."

"Irish blood never leaves you," Q said.

"Let's have no talk about blood," Maggie returned. "I want dinner."

I laid out the ingredients but was not allowed to make my soup. Maggie and Q were so overcome by hunger, and a belief that I could only cook out of tins, that they commandeered my post as head cook and banished me to the sitting room, where Aisling and I sat together and watched the darkness approach.

"So tell me," I asked. "What are your plans? Are you going back to the States?"

Aisling shrugged her shoulders. "My future is a bit up in the air, I suppose. The assistant lectureship position is mine in the fall, if I want it. It isn't a permanent position, but it might become one. Who knows? The disadvantage of taking that post is that it will last for four years and then may disappear. They call such positions 'folding chairs.'"

I laughed and crossed my legs atop a bold spring that threatened to break out of its prison inside the aging sofa.

"I'll get more money with my doctorate, and I suppose if I can write an article or two then even if the position disappears, I'll have a decent shot at another post somewhere else. It's all rather risky.

"On the other hand, if I play it safe, I still have my position at Fairview. I could return and look for a position back home. Under that scenario, I would be assured of a permanent position – even if nothing else worked out."

"But landing a college position when you're teaching high school might be more difficult."

"True. I suppose the upside potential is not as great, but then the downside potential is not as great either. I'm rather torn about it. What do you think?"

I didn't have time to express my opinion before Q came in and announced that dinner was ready.

"You know that in nouvelle cuisine the fad is to have partially cooked vegetables," Q began.

"We do have an excellent stock from the meat bones I saved," Maggie said.

"Should have cooked all afternoon," Q countered.

"If we'd waited all bloody afternoon we'd be eating tomorrow's dinner and not today's."

"I thought we weren't going to talk about blood."

Maggie laughed. I was reminded of the exhortations of her father.

"So you're all finished now," Aisling said, in an effort to turn the direction of the conversation.

Maggie and Q looked at each other. "Yes, I suppose so," Q said. "It's true. We haven't really said much about it to each other, but Maggie's going north to continue the grand tradition of Welsh school teachers in England. I'm staying here. I don't think we'll be able to carry on a relationship long distance. Deadly, that kind of thing, you know. I guess you could say we're finished."

"I meant with college, you know," Aisling put in rather quickly. Q had a habit of taking what you were saying in an odd manner.

"Oh that, too. But degrees aren't really that important, if you ask me."

"I'd never have got my job without a degree," Maggie said.

"There she goes again," Q said, directing her remarks to her audience. "Maggie's so damned practical. It's the northern Welsh air that does it to her. That and all those Welsh consonants."

"Nothing wrong with being practical. An 'idealist' is just another name for 'unemployed.'"

"I'm not unemployed," Q returned.

"No. Excuse me. You have a job with Cadit Press. Not to be confused, mind you, with Oxford University Press."

"It's a real job with a real salary. About the same as you'll be making in the northern lands of Yorkshire."

"Ah, but I have free room and board. If I didn't make any money at all, I could live on that alone."

"Alone. You've got that right. That's what you'll be. Alone."

"You make choices in life. You can't go crying over things that don't work out. Besides, there's nothing to stop you from living with me in Yorkshire."

Q made a foul noise through her nose.

"We could travel on school holidays."

"I don't get school holidays at *my* job."

"We could write."

"Writing never works. You can't hold onto a relationship long distance. Let's face facts." Q turned her head to look at Aisling and me. We were wolfing down some bread to augment the raw vegetables that were floating in a meat stock replete with globules of still-congealed fat.

"We've been around and around on this one. What's your opinion? Am I right or am I right?" Q said. She and Maggie sat expectantly for an answer.

Aisling answered for both of us, "Is this all the bread? Or did you save some uncut?"

"Rather sad what those two are going through," Aisling said as we sauntered in the direction of her place. We had already passed it twice. Neither one of us was prepared to let go of the evening. Finally, we chose to sit under a bus shelter on a little metal bar meant to give some ease to the weary.

"Each of them has an agenda for her life. Neither is willing to bend."

"That can be a problem with relationships," I said.

"Aristotle says that friends live for the best interests of each other. Therefore, they ought to be looking for ways that will first satisfy their companion."

"Well, you're the scholar. I'll defer to you."

Then a bus came and emptied out its human cargo. When they were dispersed, Aisling said, "If they would see the other person's interests as being the same as their own, then they'd find it impossible to come up with a direction in life that didn't include the other."

"Because the individual would see her interests as split. One half is her own and the other half is the other person's interest. Is that what you mean?"

"The other person's interests are a part of her own interest. The two cannot be split. That's the way it should be. But then there's always the problem of the 'free rider.'"

"Free rider?" I asked.

"Precisely. One person puts the other's interest as part of her own, but the partner doesn't reciprocate. This leads to emotional imperialism and the subjugation of one person by another."

"That's certainly very common," I said.

"All too common. It's part of my dissertation, but not really well developed. You remember Donne's *Devotions*?"

"You only told me to buy the *Songs and Sonnets*."

Aisling smiled. "I'm sure you know Meditation Seventeen. It begins with the discussion of for whom the church bell tolls and moves on to the bits about no man being an island."

"Oh yes. I know that. Vaguely. Never studied it, though."

"Well, Donne takes the whole thing one step further than I'm suggesting and makes it a principle that unites society. It ties all of our interests together."

"Pure individuality, then, would be just an illusion."

"Precisely. And therein lies one of the important problems of our modern age."

"Now you're sounding like a historian," I said. But the things that Aisling was saying to me fit exactly with the thoughts I had been having over the months. The money. The problems. Mookie. Europe. The German jail. Snowdon.

I was not as analytical a thinker as Aisling. But I could follow what she was saying, and much of what she was saying complemented the sorts of things I had been realizing on my own. In my conversation with her, it was as if I were with another part of myself that didn't pull away from me but instead made everything much stronger.

I went over our conversation, the chance meeting, the dinner, our walk – everything. In my mind I replayed the scene like a mantra until I fell asleep. A deep, sound sleep. The best sleep I had had since I could remember.

The next morning I awoke, dressed, and went downstairs to find the house deserted. I looked at the clock. It was eight thirty. Late. I was generally up by seven, or even earlier.

I didn't rush, but instead lingered over a bowl of muesli. I remembered how Father Mac always used to call muesli "gerbil food." He loved the traditional high-cholesterol breakfast of eggs, fried toast, and sausage. In England, they'd throw in some bacon too. He was a man who had made a difference in my life. When I had first come to Bethesda I was pretty apathetic about spiritual matters. I had just finished my student teaching and gotten my certification and was ready to face the world. Unfortunately, that was the problem. I was unprepared for the world I was about to face. I needed help. Father Mac lent me that help. He also helped me realize that everything we do has a consequence. Nothing is acquired without something being lost. It's all a zero sum. If I got a special prize that is worth +5, then somewhere there was an event that was −5: $5 + (−5) = 0$. The sum is always zero.

If this was so, then who got the −5? Could it be transferred to others? This was a strategy that was often employed by those moving up the ladder of success – Bernie, for example.

Another level of recognition was when that −5 happened to us. It depended upon one's outlook. I remembered a story I'd recently read in the book Q gave me: There was once a farmer whose horse ran away. The people in the village commiserated with the farmer. "Bad luck," they said. The farmer replied, "Let's wait and see." The next week, a beautiful wild horse came onto the farmer's property and the farmer captured the animal. It was more beautiful than the horse that had run away." Good luck," said the people of the village. The farmer replied, "Let's wait and see." Then the farmer's only son was thrown from the new horse and broke his ankle so that he had to walk with a permanent limp. "Bad luck," said the farmer's friends. The farmer replied, "Let's wait and see." Finally, the emperor declared a war on the Mongols and all the male children of the village had to go to war – all save the farmer's son who was exempted because he was crippled. Those village sons who went off to battle were all killed . . .

Q's gift was this tome on emptiness. Father Mac was dead. His legacy to me was an appreciation for the spiritual side of life. My biological father had left me a fortune. Yet that was a legacy that had almost destroyed me. I finished breakfast and wrote a letter. I sealed it and walked over to Aisling's flat. She was gone so I slid the note under the door. It was time to wait.

Chapter Eighteen

The next week I found myself sitting and waiting while Aisling underwent her oral defense of her dissertation. I felt like the proverbial father in a maternity waiting room. The room I was in, however, was a secretary's office. The secretary had gone to lunch so I was alone. There were no magazines, but fortunately I had brought along a paperback novel.

It was a rather plain room with old plaster walls that were cracked in a number of places. There were no pictures. Only dirty cream-colored paint. I hadn't had a chance to get a good look at the conference room in which Aisling – at that very instant – was being grilled by a committee of four scholars. Earlier I had asked her how many people passed their oral defense.

"If your committee likes your dissertation, you'll pass. They'll give you opportunities to show how much you know about your subject. And if you've done a good job, you should know quite a bit in and around the edges, so to speak."

"What if they don't like it?"

"If they don't like it, then you're probably sunk. In that case, they'll try to find out what you *don't* know. Obviously, when writing on anything, there are avenues that are touched upon slightly (or 'alluded to') but that aren't principal concentrations of yours. No one can have the knowledge necessary to defend all of these.

"A particularly bad trick is to have someone on your committee fix upon one of these 'latent minor themes' and declare it to be (or that it 'should have been') a major concentration in your dissertation. At this point, the antagonist mounts a heavy attack using this latent minor theme and demands mountains of supporting material that you don't have (because that theme was never your focus in the first place). When this happens, you can: *one*, declare the so-called theme not to be a concentration of the dissertation at all; *two*, try to give as much supporting material as you can; or *three*, admit that you can't support the theme and declare it to be one of your professional goals in the future when you begin writing journal articles.

"Now the trouble with number one is that if you deny that this latent minor theme is a theme, then your antagonist can say it should have been and you've been stupid to have missed the most important issues. Unless you successfully attack the questioner here, you'll fail with this approach. The trouble with number two is that it plays into their hands and you'll end up looking stupid and undeserving of your doctorate (and will probably fail). Number three depends upon the mercy of your inquisitors. However, if they've taken this tack in the first place, they're probably not in a very merciful mood. Number three also leads to failure.

"Thus, number one is the only hope. But there are many reasons why attacking a senior scholar is a dangerous endeavor. The best thing is for your group to be satisfied with your work in the first place."

"Is there any way to tell whether your committee likes your dissertation before you go through the inquisition?"

"If they've been honest with you all along, then you'll have a pretty good idea. But often people don't say what they really mean out of a fear of hurting your feelings, or because they don't have what it takes to be straight with you."

"You mean you could go in thinking everything will be fine and discover once the orals begin that everyone has hated your topic all along and they're just waiting to 'get you'?"

"It does happen. And I think it's more common in Britain than in the United States, because in Britain everyone in academia is so much more indirect than they are in the United States. They don't come right out and say something is a piece of trash. Instead, they tell you that your work has 'a musical narrative voice.'"

"I don't get it."

"The point is, who the hell cares about 'a musical narrative voice' unless you're writing poetry? If that's the best thing they can say about it, then they are damning it with faint praise."

"Phew. I'm glad I'm not keen on winning an English doctorate."

And so I waited. Expectant. Aisling had told me the entire process would take between two and three hours. It had already been two hours when the secretary came back. I was getting antsy. The light in the office wasn't really that good for reading. (I'd noticed that the English didn't allow themselves as much reading light as Americans. Being a person who loves to read for long intervals, I considered the illumination factor an important one.)

I left word with the secretary about where I was going and then went outside for a walk. It was a warm June day. I was sweating almost immediately. I couldn't focus my thoughts on anything except Aisling's exam.

After a few blocks I turned around and went back. I was just mounting the stairs to the second floor when I saw her. Instantly, I knew. She had passed.

"How did it go? Was it hard? Let's go for a walk. Better yet, let's go for a meal."

"It's time for tea. I know a teashop near here that has the most wonderful jams for their scones. And yes, I did. And yes, it was. Details with our tea."

I wanted to hug her, but in her arms were the books and articles that she thought she might need as supporting material. The first thing to do was to deposit them somewhere.

Aisling led me to a rather ordinary building about a block away. Like most of the university buildings I had been in, this one didn't have a lift. On the third floor was a little office located next to the ladies' WC. "Originally they offered me a nicer office, which I would have had to share with four other juniors, but I preferred to have some privacy. It's small, but it's my own."

We placed her materials in a heap on the desk and exited: light and free!

At the teashop, while the waitress was setting down our cakes, scones, jam, clotted cream, and tea, I thought of Father Mac. At the slightest excuse he would slop on a good dollop of heavy cream. "If you're going to have a treat, why not make it a treat?" he would say.

The cakes and scones were heavenly. The shop was on the second floor of the building, just above a clothing store. It consisted of twelve wooden tables that had been revarnished perhaps once too often; in the late-afternoon heat, one's arms stuck to the tabletop. The napkins were paper. But the food was divine.

"I read your note," Aisling began as she poured herself some tea.

I looked up. Her freckles seemed subdued today.

"I want to know more, before we continue," she said.

"What do you want to know?"

"Why you quit your teaching job."

"Do you want the short or the long answer?"

"Whichever you choose."

"Well, you remember when my father died?"

"Yes. You never talked about it much, but that doesn't mean it wasn't brutal for you."

"You remember how I told you that I was to come into some money, but I wasn't exactly sure how much?"

"Yes. So?"

"Well, when the money came, it triggered a chain reaction that altered my life. As a result, I found out I couldn't continue as I was. Everything short-circuited. (I'll go into the details later.) But I found myself confronted with myself. And I wasn't really prepared for that."

"And who are you, Michael?"

"The man you've been observing over the past six months."

"I see," she said and tilted her head again.

"Or, *have seen*," I retorted trying to keep up with her.

"Quite."

"Let's get on with it," I said with enthusiasm.

"That's my point. Exactly." Her head was still tilted. "Let me get this straight, so now you're living off some money that is soon to expire. You've purchased for yourself time to sort it all out."

"Yes."

"What am I to say?" She raised her palms into the air and shrugged her shoulders.

"You have my note."

"Yes. The note. Well, first let me address my situation. You know my options. There may be more. But presently those are the most apparent to me." Her head tilted even more as she said this.

"Yes."

"You've never given me your advice as to which option I should choose." Her words were ambiguous to me. I knew I wasn't clever enough to figure them out just like that. I decided to take another tack.

"Tell me, then. Do you like to teach?" I asked.

"Yes."

"Why?"

"I love the intellectual stimulation. And I enjoy the opportunity to help others discover literature." This time her words rang true to my ears.

"At what level do you most enjoy this interaction?" I wanted to know just the sort of person she had become.

"Ah, therein lies the question, doesn't it?"

"Let me digress a minute," I returned. "For *me*, the level is unimportant. I feel what you suggest, but independently. I want to *interact* with others. And at the same time I want to interact with the dead: the people who came before. When I read what they wrote, I am in *awe*. 'Life is short, Art is long.' This interaction is enough for me. I don't need anyone telling me, 'Good fellow,' 'Stout lad,' and so forth. I enjoy the interaction. But the two, *for me*, don't have to occur at the same time."

"There lies the difference between us," Aisling said. "If I were to speak truly I would have to say that I want both together. Not only that, but along with an external structure that keeps me at it."

"You know, when I was a runner in high school, I had two track coaches. The first – I don't remember his name, call him Mr. X – thought I would be a lousy runner. When I ran for him, I lived down to his expectations.

"The second was named Mr Stoll. He made me think I could do it. He challenged me to achieve beyond what I thought I could. To this day, I'll never forget Mr Stoll. A bachelor, who once served in John Kennedy's Peace Corps. He was a man who created an environment in which I could achieve. And what a feeling that was."

"Yes. I know the effects of a positive external environment. So. What's your recommendation? What do you think I should do?"

"Marry me. Stay in England. Go after your possibilities. Here."

"And what if my position goes flat?" she said as her head straightened once more.

"Well, with the money I've managed to save out of all this mess, we can supplement a modest lifestyle. But is this the real question we should be asking? Shouldn't we really be asking what style of life is the best for us both?"

"Yes. You're right. That is the question." She began to tilt her head again, but paused mid-motion and returned it straight. "And yes, I will marry you."

"You will?"

"Of course I will. And of course we must devote ourselves to each other."

"We've run out of tea."

"But we've only begun."

Aisling was given her post. And because she had done so well in her work, she was given every indication that her position would become permanent. We were married a month later.

It was a good decision to stay in London. Aisling now enjoys the life of a scholar. She is meticulous in her research and constant in her work habits. The fact that she has come into her career rather later in life than many of her colleagues has allowed her a perspective she might otherwise not have had. She is presently halfway through a shortened form of her thesis on the interrelationship between John Donne and Aristotle's metaphysics. When she is done with a section, she often will read it to me. I like it a lot, but then, I'm an expert neither in literature nor in philosophy.

We decided to live on Aisling's pay. This is the surest thing about our life. If all else fails – well, we would rethink things then. Also, it will give us more flexibility should we decide to have children.

I continue to receive the interest on the $540,000 that I had extracted from Bernie and put into a rolling certificate of deposit. And I still had some money left from my parting with Mookie. An emergency fund.

I decided that I needed a job. This took some doing, as jobs weren't overly plentiful at the time. I took a volunteer job in a literacy clinic in the East End. Positions for people who weren't looking to be paid are always easier to land. I got my hand back into teaching, and it connected me to the kinds of students who had first drawn me into the field. I had done my student teaching with people in need: poor kids who I had always felt were just as smart as anyone else, except that fewer people cared about them. Consequently, they were a little rough around the edges.

Michael Boylan

But the interaction of minds was as stimulating as any I had had at Fairview. I've made some friends from my job and have gotten preliminary support for starting a running club.

In time, Aisling helped me land a part-time paying slot at the university where she worked as research assistant to a history professor. I was one of ten bodies engaged in a long-term project to study values in Ancient Rome. With the job, I got to putter about the libraries, read articles, and continue my quest to test some of the conclusions about life that I had made since my inheritance.

At the beginning of this narrative I asked you what you would do if you suddenly became rich. In my story, I *did* become rich. It has occurred to me, of late, though, that it is impossible to *suddenly* become rich.

Think about it. It is my bequest to you.

Acknowledgments

This book has been a long time in the making: 16 years. It has had four key periods of revision. Because of this long journey there are far too many people who have helped me than I can thank directly. However, I would like to mention a few who stand out. First, I'd like to thank Charles Johnson who has stood by this project from the beginning with support and encouragement. Second are those who have assisted along the way with comments and suggestions: Robert Warburton, Daisy Blackwell, Paul Churchill, and Wanda Teays. A special thanks to Bill Haines for his help with the calligraphy. Third, I'd like to thank Jeff Dean, my editor, who took a chance on viewing a fiction narrative as philosophy. In the same vein, I'd also like to acknowledge his associate, Danielle Descoteaux, my copy-editors Jenna Dolan and Jenny Roberts, Simon Eckley and the whole team at Blackwell who have made the extra effort to make this a special project. Finally, there is my family (Rebecca, Arianne, Seán, and Éamon) who put up with me and continue to bring out the best in me.

For those readers who want to explore other ways to use this book – in the classroom or in reading groups – I invite them to visit www.blackwellpublishing.com/publicphilosophy.